Just a Groom

Laurie Twizel

Chapter One

Elsa Aldridge wiped away the bead of sweat that glistened across her forehead, and tucked a strand of loose, damp, dark caramel coloured hair behind her ear.

She felt the tears welling up again, but willed herself not to cry. She wiped her filthy hands down the sides of her jeans, and stepped back to admire her hard work. Nobby nickered and nuzzled her for treats. She stroked her palm gently over his velvet nose. Her arms ached and her palms were sore, but her horse looked stunning, and there was no way he was leaving her care looking less than a million dollars. She gave him a slice of carrot and let herself out of his stall.

"Ready?" Sophia asked solemnly, studying her. "Are you crying?"

Elsa defiantly shook her head. "No. Just got a bit of dirt in my eye."

Sophia nodded in understanding. "You'll set me off again," her boss gave a gentle laugh. "It's heart-breaking, but what can I do?" she shrugged. "His owners are well within their rights to send him where they see fit. At least they're sending me their two new youngsters."

"So that you can train them up, put in all the hard work, then they can ship them off to Frederick-*bloody*-Twemlow, too?" Elsa retaliated, unable to hide her bitterness towards the top event rider receiving their horse, who already had a stable yard bursting to the seams of high-calibre event horses. As far as she could see, two uneducated youngsters to replace the loss of a small yard's top horse was little consolation.

Sophia gave a half-hearted shrug. "It pays the bills."

Elsa nodded. Her quip was unfair; she knew Sophia was hurting just as much as she was, if not more.

Nobby was gazing at them over his stall door, wondering what all the fuss was about. He stretched out his sleek neck and nibbled on the sleeve of Elsa's jacket; on the off-chance it might be edible.

"Please, will you take him, alone?" Sophia asked, ferociously wiping her eyes.

"Of course," Elsa told her. "It's my job, and I owe it to him."

"And so do I, but I just can't face going...*there*. He's such an arrogant bastard; I don't think I could bare his snide remarks. He'll be loving it."

Elsa understood. It would be tough to keep her head held high, and her comments at bay, but she would manage it even if it killed her. She wheeled the hay wheelbarrow along the row of stables, and chucked a section of hay over each stable door, and then she was ready. There was no prolonging the inevitable any longer.

Elsa backed the lorry across the yard of the old dairy farm; Sophia's father's cows having long vacated to an upgraded milking barn across the lane to make way for Sophia's ponies, and now that she was older and taller, her horses. The old dairy barn was stacked to the rafters with hay and straw. The yard was small and characteristic, and Elsa loved it here. The single-row stable block was brick built, with an extension added later as the herd grew, of wooden built stables that were due a coat of creosote. The worn cobbled yard was replaced here and there with odd patches of ugly concrete. The yard was wonky and rugged, and was the bane of Elsa's life trying to keep it swept. But the whole yard was full of history and character.

Nobby was hyped; he was convinced he was going to a show. He had no idea of Elsa's torment as she fastened his travel boots for the last ever time, and lead him up the ramp into the lorry. He tied up obediently, stuck his nose immediately into his haynet. Nobby loved going out in the lorry – he lived for training and going to shows, and Elsa lived to get him there. Her heart felt heavy, as if suffocating her at the realisation that they'd never do that again.

Frederick Twemlow's yard was nothing but glorious, and Elsa couldn't help the stab of envy she felt as she turned onto the long, tree lined drive that passed acres of immaculate paddocks and his own cross country course, on the way down to the immaculately kept brick-built stable yard that backed on to his parent's stately home. The main yard was a horseshoe shape, with a cobbled floor and a fountain emerging from an impressive flower bed gracing the middle.

Opposite was an expansive outdoor arena that made Sophia's manège look tiny. And at the back was a huge indoor arena beside the second stable block.

With such an impressive yard, came an equally impressive rider, with a stunning string of top-class horses. Frederick Twemlow was a young rider at the top of his game, and despite despising him for snatching away the ride on Sophia's best horse; Elsa couldn't help but admire him also. Everything had been going right for him this year – win after win – and he was tipped to make the team for the next Olympics. He wanted to be the best in the world, and no one could dispute his hard work and dedication to get there.

But why her Nobby? She sighed. But she knew why, as did Sophia, and it was a real kick in the teeth to their own hard work and dedication. And when your father was an influential public figure with some fancy title, Elsa supposed you could get whatever you wanted.

She parked the lorry alongside Frederick's own huge, plush wagon, adorned with his sponsors logos all over the glistening paintwork, and with a living area probably bigger and more luxurious than Elsa's little groom's cottage. She sighed. Everything here was huge and impressive; she hoped that Nobby would want for nothing.

Frederick's groom was sweeping the yard. Ava was a petite and bubbly Australian who didn't look like she had it in her to handle half a tonne of fit event horse, but she did it impeccably and was well-respected within the eventing community. Elsa had seen her around at a few events, but had rarely spoken to her before. Frederick was in a totally different league to Sophia, but over the last couple of years Sophia had really been working hard and noticeably closing that gap. But now the departure of her top horse was a massive setback for her. Gone were any chances of getting onto the national teams; it looked like Elsa would be back to trucking around the country every weekend at the crack of dawn for Sophia to do the baby classes again.

A fresh wave of tears threatened as she let down the ramp, and she willed herself not to cry – not here. Nobby gave her a whinny, and tried to look over the partition at his new surroundings. She went everywhere with him, and he trusted her implicitly. Yet here she was about to hand him over into the unknown. It was a feeling she didn't think she could ever get used to, no matter how nice the receiving stable yard was.

Ava waved and came over, extended a dainty hand towards her with a huge smile, which at the moment Elsa didn't feel that she could even try to replicate.

"I'm Ava, pleased to meet you," she said friendlily, her Australian accent still strong, despite having been Frederick's travelling head groom for six years now.

"Elsa, likewise." Her voice was shaky. She hoped Ava had not noticed, but how could she not, and she gave Elsa a gentle understanding nod. Her friendliness knocked Elsa off guard; she'd expected that everyone at Frederick Twemlow's yard was much like him – arrogant, stuck-up with their heads shoved so far up their own arse. She tried to fight away her bitterness, but it was tough.

Nobby was pawing the ground, aware that he hadn't been here before. He was eager to get out, and Elsa swung back the partitions and went to his head.

"He's a real looker, isn't he?" Ava beamed.

Elsa nodded, not trusting herself to speak, and studied her. She was slightly older than Elsa – probably late twenties – with wispy blonde hair that she scraped back into a ponytail. She wore jeans, tatty brown boots and a polo shirt. She was tanned golden brown, with freckles dashed across her face. She looked kind and friendly, and Elsa immediately warmed a little.

"He's beautiful," Elsa told her eventually, "in both looks and nature."

"He'll fit in well here, then," Ava reassured her.

Elsa led him down the ramp, and let him look around curiously at his new surroundings. He whinnied and got a couple of replies from the occupants of the nearest stable block. He pawed the ground impatiently, and Elsa couldn't bear to hand his lead rope over.

"Would you like to show him to his new stable?" Ava offered, as if reading her mind. "Get him settled in? I'm in no hurry if you're not."

Elsa nodded eagerly. "I'd really like that, thank you."

Nobby's new stable was spacious and airy, a huge, deep bed of pristine white shavings, an automatic water drinker in the corner, and a hay rack bulging with haylage, and a haynet hung by the door. He sniffed all around it and looked extremely pleased. Ava removed his travel boots while Elsa untied the tail guard, and slipped his leather headcollar from him. Elsa had polished Nobby's brass nameplate until it sparkled. Reluctantly, she handed it to Ava, and gave her best boy a final pat.

There were sounds of hurried footsteps as she let them out of his stall.

"Where's my boy?" Christine Forrester screeched across the yard, having not yet noticed them. She was plump with dark, curly hair, and always thought herself well above the likes of Sophia and Elsa. Had she not been a much-needed owner, Elsa would not have been able to bite her tongue the many times Christine had tried to instruct Sophia how to ride Nobby better. She implored to anyone who would listen how she had been a fine three-day event rider in her youth until an injury had caused her to give up riding. But Elsa had it on good authority that she had barely even ridden before, let alone evented, but she just liked to sound important amongst her pompous friends and hang around at horse trials. *Nobby deserves better than her,* Elsa thought sadly.

Christine paused, looking around herself in delight. "Oh, isn't this stable block *marvellous!*" she clasped her hands together.

"She's here," Ava murmured, with a roll of her eyes. "That means boss'll be out in a minute, too."

"Oh, I'd better go quickly, then." Elsa said. Christine Forrester and Frederick Twemlow were the last people she wanted to see right now, and she was not inclined to make polite conversation with either of them.

"No, it's fine, you can stay. There's no hurry." Ava smiled, glad of the company.

"Honestly, I'd rather go." Elsa insisted.

"You sure? Most girls only come here to lay eyes on Frederick in the flesh." Ava commented with raised, teasing eyebrows, trying to lighten the mood.

"I'm not most girls." Elsa told her evenly, coldly holding her gaze.

"Sounds like you'd fit in well around here too, then." Ava smiled.

Elsa liked her. She couldn't help it. She felt a stab of being a traitor, to Sophia, though she would never change allegiance. But grooms had to stick together, no matter who their boss was.

Frederick Twemlow let out a low whistle as he surveyed the pretty little thing standing across his yard. She wasn't looking for him, nor looking around in awe at her surroundings. If anything, she was looking like she'd rather be anywhere else in the world right now, and the sight of her left him feeling intrigued.

"Nobby has one of the best stables in the yard, Mrs Forrester," came Frederick's smooth superior voice, appearing as if from nowhere and making Elsa jump.

Elsa couldn't help but look. He was tall, tanned, authoritative and truly gorgeous, with a treasure trove of soft blonde curls, and piercing blue eyes. He had a beauty that made any female stop in her tracks and just stare at him in admiration. No wonder he held the approval of every eventing-crazy female across the country – he really was very easy on the eye. Even more so in the flesh than the many times she had examined him on the big screen at the horse trials. She nervously bit her bottom lip as she stole a look at him close-up. Even Christine Forrester was blushing under his gaze, and Elsa was glad he hadn't noticed her. She expected to be able to slip away unnoticed, and she slowly stepped back. She knew *he* wouldn't even so much as look in the direction of someone like *her*.

"I am *so* looking forward to working with you," Christine Forrester was babbling on. "This is *such* a good opportunity for both you *and* Nobby; he is truly an *amazing* horse."

Elsa involuntarily rolled her eyes, and Ava smiled.

"She's all yours now," Elsa told her quietly, as the pair backed away. "And for that, I am not sad."

Ava nodded in silent agreement. Nobby munched on his haynet, oblivious. He had finished sniffing all around his new box, and seemed satisfied. The big gelding didn't care who owned him, so long as there was a constant supply of food.

Frederick neared, and his gaze flitted across Nobby and fell on her. He nodded politely, and Elsa already felt herself shrinking before him.

"You must be his groom?" he enquired, not smiling. She was trying to look anywhere but *at* him, and he concealed his amusement. Most girls he engaged with made any excuse to trail a hand down his arm and flutter their eyelashes at him, but this groom's behaviour was...*refreshing*.

"I was," Elsa mumbled, stopping in her tracks. *Stand tall,* she abruptly told herself, refusing to crumble under his intimidating, straight posture. She cleared her throat and squared her shoulders. "Take good care of him, won't you? He'll be missed."

"Sophia is a capable young rider," Christine was going on. "But he wasn't reaching his full potential there. We really believe he could be a four-star horse. She was so *slow* with his progress, you know?" She had hold of Frederick's arm, imploring with him. But Frederick wasn't really listening; his gaze was still settled on Elsa.

"We will. Can I..." he began.

"I have to go," Elsa cut him off, not wanting to hear anything he had to say. She could barely trust herself to speak, and couldn't meet his eye. She went to turn away.

"Does my groom have your number?" he frowned, his abruptness stopping her.

She nodded. "I wish you the best of luck with him," she croaked, and turned on her heel.

"I'll show you out," Ava called after her, and jogged to catch up.

Elsa wanted to be left alone. She could manage it across the yard to her lorry without anyone escorting her, but Ava was persistent.

"He's my best friend," Elsa explained feebly, wiping the tears from her eyes. She pulled her jacket tighter around her, even though she wasn't cold.

Ava nodded in understanding.

"God, I feel so stupid!"

"Don't feel stupid." Ava gently put her arm around her shoulder. "The good ones get under your skin, don't they? If we didn't feel emotion there's no way we'd be doing this job."

"Thanks for being so nice," Elsa smiled.

"Why would I not be nice? You're young," Ava laughed, reaching down to help her lift the ramp. "During the course of your career, lots of good horses will come, and lots will go. That's life."

Elsa forced a smile. The ramp was fastened, and she was ready to go.

"Please call me, any time, if you have any concerns about him. He's very special to me."

Ava nodded. "He'll have the best care here."

Elsa bit her lip. *He had the best care at ours; he shouldn't be leaving.* She nodded. "Right, see you around." She climbed up into the cab and hastily started the engine, desperate to get out of here.

She drove back with blurred vision; the tears refusing to subside. She felt drained of all energy as she struggled to change gears on the lorry. The clutch was so heavy, she felt so weighed down with a feeling of loss. Normally driving the lorry was such a happy time – going to a show, or coming home no matter how good or bad it had gone. If they'd had a successful day, the drive home was joyful and easy. If it had gone bad, it was always a good time for reflection and action planning. Only if they were returning with an injured horse was the journey sombre. But this was a lonely, empty journey, with no positives for Elsa to grasp hold of.

The yard was quiet when she parked the lorry up. She let down the ramp and began sweeping out the soiled shavings while she could still muster any enthusiasm. Bear gave her an impatient whinny as she passed her box on her way to the muck heap, and Elsa knew she should saddle her up and head off down the fields, but she was worn out.

The little chestnut nuzzled her pockets as she let herself into her box, and she didn't let her down as she produced a slice of carrot for her.

"You're spoilt," Elsa told her, giving her face a good rub. Bear nodded against her palm.

"Horse walker for you today, I'm afraid. I promise I'll take you out tomorrow."

And then she could get on with mucking out Nobby's stall, ready for whoever was to next occupy the prime position on the yard. She might as well get it done right away; she had to get used to him not being here.

It was getting late by the time she had finished on the yard, and she checked one last time that all the horses had hay and water before letting herself back into her cottage. Her stomach grumbled to remind her she had not eaten all day. She was so hungry, but the day had been so draining she wasn't sure she could muster the energy to even drag herself to the kitchen, let alone to raid the cupboards and rustle up something to eat.

Elsa's little cottage was homely and perfect for her. Destined for the workers when the dairy farm had been in its heyday, it was a simple, cosy two-up two-down. Barely enough room to swing a cat, let alone Elsa's leggy Lurcher-cross-deerhound Cecil, who took up most of the space.

From her small kitchen window she could see the heads of all her charges looking out over their stable doors, and from the living room patio doors she could look out across the valley and watch the dairy cows grazing alongside Sophia's young, as yet unbroken horses each with a very bright future.

She went straight through to the living room and flopped down on the sofa, not caring for the bits of hay and straw she trailed behind her. It was on days like this that she was glad she lived alone.

Even though the interior of Elsa's cottage was quite plain, she had done her best to put her own stamp on it and make it homelier. Opposite her was the fireplace; a lifesaver from the cold of winter when she had been outside all day – for both warming herself and Cecil, and drying her endless gloves and coats – but somewhat redundant during these summer months. Along the mantelpiece were old, faded photos of a young Elsa on her cherished pony, and tacked all around the big, oblong mirror. But in pride of place in the centre of the mantelpiece, was a framed, professional photo of Sophia and Nobby tackling their first ever three-star. Sophia was clearing the huge ditch in style, Nobby's ears were pricked and he looked a million dollars.

Elsa had cried tears of joy that day when she'd collected him from the finish; she'd been so relieved that both of them had got around safely. They'd always known Nobby was special, and thanks to him, people had really started to take notice of Sophia as a serious contender for future titles. And God knew she deserved it. It was just a shame that her fellow, more influential competitors had to notice just how good her horse was, too.

She switched on the TV and fumbled around on the floor by the sofa for her emergency bottle of red wine, taking a swig straight from the bottle. Cecil gazed up at her through big, brown eyes, a look of disapproval etched across his shabby face.

"I know, Cecil," she rubbed the grey, long-legged, shaggy creature affectionately behind the ears. "But it's been a shit day. Let's curl up with an equally shitty film, and you can watch me polish off this bottle, hey?"

He yawned, and spun his attention quickly to the front door. He barked instantly before the doorbell rang. Elsa groaned and dragged herself to her feet. She hoped there was nothing wrong with any of the horses; they'd all been fine when she'd checked them, and she couldn't cope with any more trauma today.

Petra Hamilton stood on the doorstep, a casserole pot balanced in her oven-gloved hands.

"Sorry to intrude," Sophia's mother smiled. "But I thought you probably hadn't eaten."

Elsa could have kissed her. "Of course you're not intruding; you're the best boss *ever!*"

"Don't be silly." Her tamed, blonde curls bounced off her shoulders. "Will you eat it?"

"Of course I'll eat it." Elsa's stomach rumbled in anticipation. "Please, come in."

Cecil sniffed hopefully at the pot and his long, thick tail slapped against the kitchen cabinets. Petra easily located a plate and cutlery, and dished the casserole up as all Elsa could seem to do was lean helplessly on the back of the kitchen chair and watch.

"You look exhausted," Petra commented gently. "I assumed you'd be in the same low spirits as Sophia. It is a blow."

Elsa felt the fresh tears pricking her tired eyes, and willed them away.

"But you're both tough cookies; you'll pick each other up."

Elsa nodded, not trusting herself to speak. What was wrong with her? Horses came and went; it was part of the job. She knew that. Some were good, some were bad, but none of them affected her as much as Nobby had.

"He was pretty special to me," she murmured. "There was something about him. He and Sophia were going to go all the way."

"And he still will, hopefully, but with someone else. No matter how bitter we are about it, be thankful that he is fit and well. Anything could have happened; he could have fallen lame and Sophia lose her top horse that way. She's a fighter, and she needs you to pick her back up again. We have some really nice young horses here, and it's time for one or two of them to step up to the mark."

Elsa nodded. She knew that Petra was right. Petra was always right. She was the real boss around here, the voice of reason. She was the one that picked them up when things were down, and kept them grounded on the rare occasions things were looking too good. She lived to keep her daughters' eventing dream alive.

Dinner was quickly served. Petra pulled out a chair for her and passed her a fork.

"Eat," she told her sternly.

Elsa took her place. Cecil whined, willing some food to fall to the floor so he could claim it.

"This is delicious," she managed through hungry mouthfuls. "Thank you *so* much."

"You're very welcome. Why don't you take this weekend off, hit the town and let your hair down? I can look after things here."

"You're going to have to look after things here anyway," Elsa replied, shaking her head. "In the last two minutes, I've made the executive decision that we are taking Drop Kick to Napier this weekend, to run in the Intermediate. He's entered, and Sophia's been debating it for days, so I've made the decision."

Petra's eyes widened. "Is he ready?"

Elsa shrugged. "I hacked him this morning; he felt great. He's been storming around the Novice courses. You said it yourself; it's time for them to step up."

Petra slowly nodded, looking thoughtful.

"I'm just so angry that we, as a team, can put *so* much effort into turning a gangly-legged ugly duckling three-year-old with four left hooves, into a beautifully balanced, clean jumping, dressage swan, and have someone just take that away from you in the blink of an eye." Elsa went on.

"I know," Petra agreed softly. "But he was never ours."

"If there's one consolation, it's that I won't miss Christine Forrester storming around the place," Elsa retorted.

"I know. If she sends Sophia any youngsters, she won't visit – she has little interest in them."

"Until they're showing Olympic potential, and she can ship them off to someone else?"

Petra silently agreed.

"But why *him*?" Elsa whined. "Why Frederick-bloody-Twemlow? He already has all the horsepower that he needs!"

"Oh, Elsa, come on! Why not? You've seen him, haven't you?"

"Yes," Elsa scowled.

"Well, he probably only had to flutter his gorgeous golden eyelashes at Christine Forrester, to get her eating out of his palm. Everyone falls for his charm, Elsa. No one is immune to those looks."

"I am." Elsa replied defiantly, arms folded across her chest. She refused to acknowledge that his very presence in that barn earlier had stopped her in her tracks. Before she'd come to her senses, of course.

"No," Petra laughed. "Not even you."

Chapter Two

Elsa bolted the stall door and looked up in admiration as Drop Kick gazed out over the half door of the best stable on the yard. She couldn't think of a more deserving predecessor to Nobby's old stall than the gorgeous grey.

"You've got some big shoes to fill," she told the gentle giant, giving his cheek a scratch. "But I know you can do it."

He pawed at the ground impatiently, banging noisily against the wooden stable door.

"It'll also help keep the noise down around here," Elsa told him from under raised eyebrows. "Being next to the feed room, you'll get fed first now, OK? So less of that banging, please."

He immediately stopped banging, and she smiled. His head disappeared back over his door as he went in search of his haynet.

Beep beep. Her mobile phone chirped in her pocket.

She leant against the broom as she retrieved her phone from her jeans pocket. It was probably just a long-lost friend asking if she was still alive as they hadn't seen her forever, or even her mother. But that was what working with horses did; they took over your life.

She frowned at the number that she did not recognise.

Hi, sorry to trouble you. Nobby hasn't been eating up, and I wondered if it was anything you could help with? Frederick.

Her frown deepened as she read it over again. Nobby had never had a problem eating; she could have sworn he was a pig in a previous life. *Frederick?* Seriously, she wondered, was it *the* Frederick, or someone playing a stupid joke? Surely Frederick, with his supply of grooms, didn't personally text other people's grooms to enquire about a horse not eating?

She sighed and ran her hand through her loose caramel hair. Why the hell would *Frederick* text her himself – surely his staff oversaw feeding? And why should she help him, anyway, after everything he had done to them? But her heart panged for Nobby. Four days he'd been gone now, if he really wasn't eating he'd be uncomfortable and grumpy. He could be ill. She had a duty of care towards him, if she genuinely could help, but she also had a contractual duty to keeping Sophia's yard running, and she still had a mountain of jobs to get done *and* she'd promised Bear she'd take her on a hack.

She went to the tack room and defiantly pulled her saddle down from its rack amongst the organised clutter of leatherwork and dressage and jump saddles stacked high to the rafters. Nobby was not her responsibility anymore, and Bear needed her. She'd let her progress with Bear drop recently while she and Sophia had been travelling further to the bigger shows to try and get Nobby the exposure they both needed. And hadn't that backfired. She'd hack Bear and then maybe if she had time after she'd completed her jobs, just *maybe* she would call in and see Nobby.

She dropped her saddle down on the yard fence and turned towards the paddock. Bear was galloping the length of it, showing her athleticism in a display of bucks and plunges and high kicks as she went. She was working up a sweat and there was no way she'd be calm enough to stand and be saddled for a while.

Elsa sighed. That fiery mare was such a drama queen; she didn't know why she loved her so. But she loved to see her frolicking and just being a horse. She wondered if Nobby were being turned out in the Twemlow's plush paddocks, or whether the paddocks were just for show and the horses were all kept permanently in stalls and wrapped up in cotton wool. She hoped he was able to gallop around like a loon, but if he wasn't eating she doubted that. She sighed and put her saddle back on its rack. Maybe she would just quickly call and see

Nobby, and then by the time she returned Bear would be calm enough to hack.

She pulled into the yard, parked her little battered Fiat beside the huge plush lorry, and suddenly felt very small and inferior. She felt so out of place here, and wished she'd changed her t-shirt at least before coming here, to a clean one free from slobber and horse hair. She'd swapped her tatty yard boots for trainers before she'd left, but even they'd seen better days. She bet Frederick's staff were dressed generously by his endless list of sponsors. Elsa couldn't wait for Sophia to reach those dizzying heights.

Elsa saw Ava across the yard, sweatsheets swung across both arms as she paused from her jobs and chatted with another groom. Even though the sun had barely showed its face today, Ava wore tiny shorts and a tank top, her bronzed legs filling Elsa with envy. She turned and saw Elsa, and smiled with a mix of recognition and confusion as she chucked the sweatsheets down and walked to meet her

"Hey!" she called. "Back so soon?"

"Yea," Elsa went to her. "I got Frederick's text about Nobby not eating up."

"Huh?" Ava frowned in confusion. "Nobby's a trooper; taking it all in his stride. Eating us out of house and home."

Elsa stopped, suddenly feeling embarrassed. "But..."

"How would Frederick know anyway?" Ava laughed, cutting her off as though she were being absurd. "I've fed the last couple of days."

Elsa felt her heart rate rising. "So, I've driven all the way over here for a wind up? I'm too tired for this shit." She told her, annoyed. "What is his bloody problem?"

"Hang on a minute. He did come out earlier, asked if anything was up with Nobby. I was surprised he asked, I told him he was fine but that your number was on the whiteboard in the tack room, so I could call you if needed." She narrowed her eyes. "Give me your phone. Are you sure it was Fred?

This isn't really his style."

Frowning, Elsa took her phone from her pocket, and showed Ava the text.

Ava's face suddenly lit up. "No way! He seriously text you! That's definitely his number!"

Elsa felt her anger growing. "Seriously, does he know how much I have to do back at the yard? He's got Sophia's best horse, why can't he just leave us alone? Doesn't he realise how painful this is for us?"

"I don't think this is to get one over on you, Elsa," she replied quietly. Although what it was, she wasn't too sure of herself, either.

"Well, what is it then?" she snapped. "I've got two young horses to prepare for their first inter at the weekend."

"Oh! Are you going to Napier?" Ava asked excitedly, ignoring her question.

Elsa nodded. OK, so Sophia currently only had one horse ready to tackle intermediate classes, but she struggled admitting that even to herself, let alone to others. *We will get there,* she told herself. *We'll pick ourselves back up.*

"Us too!" Ava beamed. "We're taking Nobby and a few others."

"Is that supposed to make me feel better?" Elsa retorted.

Ava shrugged. She bit her lip, waiting.

"Sorry, it's not your fault." Elsa sighed, running her hand through her hair. "It's just I'm so tired, and this is hard enough without stupid little mind games. I didn't sweep the yard before I left, it's a pigsty compared to here. I haven't made up tonight's feeds and haynets yet, I have two manes to pull, *and* I still have to ride," she broke off, her exasperation evident. "Oh, forget it, I have to get back."

"Would you like to see him before you go?"

"Frederick?" Elsa screwed her face up in disgust. "No, thanks!"

"Not Frederick," Ava grinned. "You've made it clear how

you feel about him! He's gone out, anyway. I meant Nobby."

"Try and stop me!" Elsa immediately perked up at the thought of giving her best boy a cuddle and a carrot, especially if there was no chance of bumping into Frederick, but his strange text was not easily forgotten.

Wednesday was Elsa's favourite day at the yard, at precisely quarter to eleven when Merlin's owner Rosie pulled in ready for their hack at eleven.

"What a glorious morning!" Rosie called, as she climbed out from her Mini. "Although every morning that I come here is glorious in my eyes!"

Elsa smiled. Rosie was her favourite owner, and she loved the hacks they shared.

Rosie's husband, Ernie, was friends with Sophia's father Colin, and when he had heard through Colin one evening over a pint of ale at the local that Sophia was having to sell Merlin to pay off a vet's bill, he had kindly purchased half of him. Not a great deal of money was obtained for a green horse, but enough that kept him in Sophia's yard, and Ernie's weekly contributions towards his upkeep meant that Merlin could get out to events. Seeing him get on so well with Sophia had spurred Rosie back into the saddle after a long break, and while she was yet to find the confidence to climb aboard wayward Merlin, she indulged in a weekly lesson astride one of Sophia's more trustworthy steeds. She loved nothing more than to follow Sophia and Merlin's progress, and as long as there was a beer tent also in attendance, they could be guaranteed to be cheering him on at every event. Elsa always found events much more enjoyable with Rosie and Ernie in attendance, and they couldn't wait to watch him make the step up to Novice at Napier this weekend.

Napier was one of Elsa's favourite events, and she was looking forward to watching Sophia's now top two horses raise their game. Rain was threatened, but for now it was staying warm, and they'd even had to water the course to prevent the ground being too hard.

Elsa bathed the horses and got the lorry ready Thursday afternoon. Drop Kick was the filthiest horse she knew, and she suspected he went out of his way to get himself especially dirty just before a show, because he loved bath-time so much. As she ran the hose over his thick, grey tail, she was sure he had more shit in it than she'd mucked out of his stable. Stable stains were the bane of her life with the greys, and no matter how many rugs and bandages Drop Kick had on him, he still managed to cover himself in stains. Elsa's arms ached by the time she had scrubbed them with shampoo, and held the bucket of warm, soapy water up to soak his grimy tail.

He turned his neck around to watch her, his inquisitive ears pricked.

"Yea, you enjoy yourself, boy!" she told him fondly. "No one else gets this treatment, you know? Because no one else needs it, only you!" She pointed an accusing finger at him, and he tried to nibble it, ever hopeful that she might produce something edible.

Elsa drove the lorry down first thing on Friday morning, with Sophia and Petra arriving by car a bit later. They'd spend the Friday morning getting the horses acclimatised with the surroundings. While Drop Kick took most of the events in his stride, his younger companion tended to be a bit scatty. Merlin had low mileage as far as competing was concerned, and Elsa liked to give him ample time to settle down before the start of the competition. Sophia liked to find a quiet part of the event ground to lunge them first before she climbed aboard. She gave them regular yet short bursts of schooling throughout the event, choosing a different spot of the estate each time and often doing some pole work to get them to concentrate on the job in hand and ensure they were fully listening to her.

Elsa located the stabling they'd been allocated in the main barn, and got her two charges settled in, and then she just had to find *him*. She couldn't wait any longer to lay her eyes on that gorgeous face, and she looked on the list to find Frederick Twemlow's stable allocations.

"Nobby!" she beamed as she dashed down the aisle, not even needing to check the number on his door; she'd spot that beauty from a mile off.

He whinnied at her and she felt her heart swell with pride, and slipped him a sneaky carrot slice.

"Don't tell your new mum about that," she whispered, scratching his chin. "She might not approve." But he'd always feel like *her* horse, and she felt both pleased and a little jealous that he looked so well. "I hope they're looking after you, boy," she murmured, but she knew Frederick's horses got the best care. His staff might come and go and find many faults with their employer, but very few found fault with the horse care, and any that did were usually jealous of the outstanding facilities and regime.

She gave him a parting pat, sad that stolen moments with her best horse, in the barn away at events, were all that they shared now. Grooms hurried past her carrying hordes of equipment as they organised their charges, and she saw Ava approaching from the other end of the barn, laden down with saddles and bridles and looking flustered. She did not notice Nobby's visitor when she came to a halt three stables away.

"Oh *no!*" she let out an anguished cry, and Elsa tentatively joined her in peering over the stable door. The grey occupant was hideously dirty and his ripped rug and bandages lay scattered around his filthy stable.

"I can't believe this!" Ava groaned, wanting to cry. "I only bathed him last night, and I have three others to get ready for dressage today, too!"

"Is FT being a bit stingy on his grooms?" Elsa asked, chewing her bottom lip.

"She left." Ava sighed. "Left me all alone – or he fired her – I'm not sure which but she was useless anyway."

"No temporary ones willing to step in last minute?" Elsa asked, surprised. "Not even for FT?"

"Apparently, none that can actually *groom*," Ava rolled her eyes. "Plenty of offers from eyebrow flutterers and skimpy shorts models." She deposited the saddles and quickly untangled the leatherwork.

"OK, well," Elsa took a deep breath. "Can I help?"

"Don't you have any of your own to get ready?" Ava frowned, pausing only momentarily.

"Not for the three day, no. We only had Nobby, and he's yours now," Elsa replied, not meaning to sound bitter. "We've only brought youngsters to the one day classes; we're here early to acclimatise them."

"It's sweet of you," Ava sighed, obviously feeling guilty. "But it's my problem."

"Nonsense! Come on," Elsa replied, quickly locating a bucket and shampoo. "I have plenty of experience in bathing filthy greys, so I feel your pain. But, better than that, I have an array of magic potions to remove the toughest of stains."

"You sound like a carpet cleaning advert," Ava laughed, opening the stall door so her new groom could enter. "Thank you so much, I owe you!"

"No bother," Elsa waved her away. "Just keep it in mind when I next turn up at an event having forgotten Sophia's girths or something vital like that!"

"I shall be sure to return the favour," Ava called over her shoulder, scurrying down the aisle.

An hour and a half later, and not only was the grey meticulously clean, but Elsa also had him dried, brushed and plaited up, as she knew that was how Frederick would want him. Ava had not had a chance to check on her as she brushed and plaited her other three – another for the two-star dressage and two in the smaller classes that morning – but she could not hide her delight when she eventually peered over the stable door. Elsa didn't even catch what the grey's name was, but he was sweet. He was as quiet as a lamb, who obviously just enjoyed getting filthy and box walking in the early hours.

"Thank you *so* much," she implored again. "You are literally a lifesaver. Any time you need a favour, seriously, give me a shout!"

"Good luck today!" Elsa called, waving it away as nothing, as she let herself out the stall. She was just glad to help. "I'll catch up with you later!"

Drop Kick had his dressage test scheduled for Friday afternoon, with his show jumping and cross country the following morning – often the norm with one day events that attracted a lot of entries – while Merlin had all three phases on the Sunday, by which point Elsa hoped he would no longer be excited by his surroundings. Elsa had ample time to wash and plait Drop Kick, even taking him for a hack around the estate before handing him over to Sophia to be worked in anything to try and trick the gelding that his dressage test was not imminent. Dressage was not Drop Kick's strongest phase, and his test was average. He was lazy on the flat, and it was always a struggle for Sophia to get him to put in enough effort, but he always redeemed himself with his show jumping and cross country.

Having cooled Drop Kick off and returned him to the barn, Elsa stood at the rail to the warm up to the neighbouring ring, watching as Frederick and Nobby prepared for their two-star dressage test. She had been surprised to hear he'd be out so soon when Ava had told her, but he was going well and looked happy and healthy which was all that mattered. The pair was executing a beautiful, collected canter and Frederick seemed so in the zone that she didn't feel guilty for gawping at him.

He looked immaculate; his tall, straight posture and beautiful tailcoat, everything about him made a girl go weak at the knees. Even in the warm up he accumulated quite a crowd. Young females followed him around everywhere at events like this, admiring his muscular physique and wondering what it took to get his attention. Elsa had always wondered herself; she'd admired him until Christine Forrester had announced that he had demanded to have Nobby on his yard, and simply how could one turn down an offer like that? Elsa scowled; she had always been put off by his arrogance anyway.

Frederick noticed her as soon as she came to the ringside; that pretty, inconspicuous groom who had been somewhat on his mind ever since she had stepped foot in his stable yard. Nobby's stride did not even alter despite his rider losing some concentration as he studied his new spectator from the corner of his eye. There was something about her that he could not quite put his finger on. She looked so effortlessly pretty, yet so casual in her jeans and tatty t-shirt, her battered rucksack slung over her shoulder, like she really did not want to stand out. But she did stand out, *to him*. Nobby flicked his ears, as if suddenly noticing his rider wasn't really with him, and Frederick knew his own behaviour was rather unusual; he was normally one hundred percent committed to his horse. But he finally seemed to have this groom's attention – despite her eyes almost certainly only being fixed on him because he was riding Nobby – but he would use that it to his advantage. He had an important question that needed to be asked.

He pulled to a halt beside her, did a perfect rein back and turned to look at her. "Elsa..." he purred, in that smooth voice that made females *melt*. She jumped out of her skin, and gawped helplessly further.

She looked quickly around her to see who else he could be referring to, as surely it couldn't be her. But she was alone. He *remembered* her? He remembered her *name*. She hadn't expected him to notice her, thought she could gawp freely, unnoticed.

"Hi," she croaked, embarrassed. She wanted to give him a piece of her mind for leading her on a wild goose chase with that strange text and Nobby's phantom ailments, that had been bugging her ever since she'd made the unnecessary trip to his yard, but all of her strength vaporised before him.

"Nobby is feeling good." He smiled, and she wondered if he were taunting her.

"He looks amazing," she admitted, reluctantly. "I wasn't expecting to see him out so soon."

"He is fit, healthy, well-schooled, and raring to go." He shrugged, as if he couldn't quite believe it himself. "I figured, why not?"

She nodded and defiantly held his gaze. "All our horses are like that."

"Testament to all your hard work," he smiled, his brilliant blue eyes looking right at her.

Elsa wasn't sure she could cope with compliments from someone who definitely wasn't known for giving them, whether he meant it or not. And her loyalty to Sophia told her that she certainly did not want them.

"Well, I'll let you get on," she turned away, his inquisitive gaze unnerving her.

"I wondered," he began cautiously, stopping her. "To show that there are no hard feelings between us, would you let me buy you dinner this evening?"

Elsa's eyes widened in surprise. "Isn't it Sophia, that you should be showing there are no hard feelings?" she smiled sweetly. She didn't need or want his sympathy, either. "I'm just the groom, after all."

"But it's not Sophia I want to share dinner with." He told her, amused.

Elsa could hear her heart beating fast. Had she just heard him properly? He wanted to buy *her* dinner? The most eligible bachelor on the circuit, who had endless pretty girls flocking after him desperate to be taken to dinner, and he'd asked *her*.

And he didn't look like he was teasing. He didn't look like he felt particularly sorry for her, either. She frowned. Surely he wasn't human? She knew he definitely hadn't looked at her properly. He was always turned out immaculately – on and off a horse – and here she stood in faded jeans all frayed around the hem, faded brown boots that were meant to be dark brown, a grubby white t-shirt with a hoof oil stain across the front and grass stains up the side from where she'd been rolling around on the lawn with Cecil. She had more hay than hair in her ponytail. She couldn't meet his eye without feeling her cheeks reddening.

Slowly, she shook her head. "I can't. I'm too busy," she croaked, her eyes flitting around to look anywhere but at *him*.

He nodded, trying to hide his disappointment. "I understand. Maybe some other time, then?"

He looked vaguely bemused, and she resisted the temptation to poke her tongue out at him. Frederick Twemlow was probably used to getting his own way. Being that good looking, she suspected you'd have to be mad to turn him down. Maybe she was, she shrugged, but she assumed he must just feel sorry for her. Probably thought he could wine her and dine her, get her into bed, show her a good time and then everyone would be happy. *Oh no.* She knew that probably worked on many other girls who trawled after him, but not Elsa. She knew she was doing the right thing; she didn't need his pity. Plus, she couldn't be a traitor to Sophia.

He watched her back until she disappeared from him, with a gentle, puzzled shake of his head. He nudged Nobby on, and picked up his perfect collected canter as if she'd never stopped him.

She hung back as he entered the collecting ring. She didn't want him to see her following him, but when she had seen *Noble Charmer* on the start card she had left her stable jobs and rushed down here especially. Elsa watched as Ava ran a cloth around Nobby's mouth to wipe away the froth, splashed another layer of hoof oil on him, and gave him a final brush over. No one could deny he didn't look fantastic. But it didn't stop the pang at Elsa's heart that told her that it should be she, Sophia and Nobby in there right now. Ava looked up and saw her, shoved her groom's essentials back into her rucksack and came over.

"Hey!" she beamed excitedly. "Doesn't he look fab?"

Elsa nodded. "He loves it here."

"Yea, he settled in great!" Ava told her.

The bell rang, signalling for Frederick to start. He trotted around the outside a couple of times to compose himself, and then entered. Both girls watched the test in silence, only gasping in unison at the miscommunication during the extended trot, and a slightly wonky half pass to the right. The rest was flawless, and they turned down the centre line and gave a perfect square halt, and Frederick tipped his hat towards the judges.

Test completed, Frederick threw his reins down and gave Nobby a hearty pat.

"Fred will be kicking himself for those mistakes," Ava shook her head. She anxiously bit her bottom lip as they watched Frederick walk towards them.

"He is human then, after all?" Elsa commented dubiously. "Makes mistakes just like the rest of us."

"Of course he's human!" Ava replied, amused. "You're not that fond of him, are you? Must be about the only female who's not!"

"Yea, well," Elsa shrugged, desperate to get away as Fred was fast approaching. "I need to get back. Catch you later!"

Ava's attention was turned to Nobby. She took his reins as Frederick swung from the saddle, and she walked her horse away to cool off. Frederick waited, and watched after the other hastily departing figure that had again caught his eye. He could have kicked himself; those mistakes had been totally his fault. He never, *ever* lost concentration in competitions.

What the hell had he been thinking, asking someone out for dinner just before going into the ring, when he was meant to be focusing, especially someone who had turned him down! But her refusal had only made him more determined to get to know her.

Chapter Three

Elsa put headcollars on Merlin and Drop Kick, and led them outside for a pick of fresh grass. She'd finished their stables and the time was now hers. The sun was shining, and she'd donned her shorts and vest top, desperate for her pale skin to get some sort of a tan before autumn appeared.

"Fancy some company?" came an Aussie voice, and Elsa spun around to greet Ava, with Nobby on the end of her lead rope.

"Hey!" Elsa beamed at the pair of them. "Of course!"

Merlin and Drop Kick lifted their heads to whinny at their old stable mate, but were quickly distracted by the grass.

"How did your other horse go?" Elsa asked politely.

"Fred and Cavalier were absolutely flawless," Ava smiled. "They're leading the class."

Elsa tried to feel delighted for her, but it was a struggle. There was no better feeling as a groom, than to see your cherished horses doing well.

"This one didn't do too badly in his class, either," Ava rubbed Nobby's neck. "Aside from Fred's mistakes, the judges thought highly of the other movements."

"I'm glad to hear it," Elsa told her honestly.

They stood in silence, just the quiet sounds of their horses cropping grass, the occasional hustle and bustle from the lorry park. The stables were tucked away beyond the lorry park, offering peace and quiet.

"What's he like?" Elsa eventually asked, her curiosity getting the better of her.

"Who?" Ava frowned.

"Frederick." Elsa said his name with some difficulty. She wasn't sure how to feel about him anymore. Before meeting

31

him, all she'd heard about him was his arrogance, yet he was well respected on the circuit. But he clearly knew what he wanted and didn't care who he trod on to get it.

"He's focused. He doesn't let people walk all over him. He's firm, but fair." Ava shrugged. "Nice to his horses, nice to his staff. We're always looking for grooms, if you're ever interested?"

"I'd have thought you'd have grooms queuing up," Elsa muttered sub consciously. "He's a stunner."

"He's not interested." Ava replied, amused. "Girls come and go; think they can flutter their eyelashes at him. But if they can't groom, they go. No exceptions. He's a professional. I get my head down, work hard, and I'm rewarded well. Not in the same way as some girls think," she grinned. "I'm only in it for the horses. And let's face it; I'm in the best yard to work with the best horses."

Yes, Elsa thought, *you have Nobby.*

Elsa climbed up into the lorry, hoping for a sit down and a bite to eat. Cecil was stretched out across her bed. She scooped the lanky ball of shaggy hair up in her arms and kissed his forehead. She held him on her lap as she stole the warm spot he'd left on her bed. He yawned and she winced at the dog breath that protruded from between his sharp teeth. She let out a large sigh. To think, instead she could be pulling on a nice dress and joining Frederick Twemlow for dinner, if only he'd really meant it, of course.

Most girls would jump at the chance of that, and she'd declined. He probably wasn't used to rejection. She wondered if he'd even look at her now. He wasn't one known for his socialising and good character, he was here to do a job, and he simply got on with it.

Sophia was pacing the lorry. She stopped, and looked at Elsa, breaking her from her thoughts.

"That line, between the brushes." She said simply. "It's

troubling me."

Elsa nodded in understanding. "I'm sure it'll ride nicer than it walks. What did Derek say about it?"

Sophia bit her lip, unconvinced. "He said it'll ride better than it walks." She replied, and Elsa smiled. Derek was Sophia's trainer, having himself competed internationally when he was younger, he now spent his days helping his pupils get onto the national teams.

Sophia was not normally this nervous, but Drop Kick and Merlin hadn't vast experience at riding at this level. Especially with losing Nobby, there was a lot of pressure on her to do well and show that she was up to it. She went to the door and pulled on her boots.

"I'm going to walk it again." She said.

Elsa nodded. "Want me to come with?"

Sophia shook her head, and turned with a smile. "There's no need. It's probably just me being silly. But, you know..."

She trailed off, and Elsa nodded, watching as she let herself out.

Elsa's stomach rumbled and Cecil looked at her expectantly. Elsa wasn't sure now if she was proud of herself or angry for not accepting Frederick Twemlow's offer of dinner. She wondered where he would have taken her, whether he would have expected anything more of her afterwards... She wondered whether he really was just being polite, or whether there was more in it. But his behaviour towards her was not becoming of what she had heard about his character. All this wondering was killing her; she'd know the answers if she'd just said *yes*.

Elsa sighed and dragged herself back onto her feet. Cecil whined and pattered to the door. She grabbed his lead off the hook and swung open the door to be met by rain. So much for a weekend of fine weather, she thought, the dreaded rain had finally come. It always amazed her how the weather could turn so quickly. Always prepared, she tugged her waterproof coat and wellies on.

She took Cecil for a walk through the woodland that buttered the main road from the lorry park. He quickly got hold of the scent of a rabbit, and scurried off in the undergrowth. The ground was wet and squelchy, and the smell of damp wood and leaves was strong.

Once Cecil gave up chase and returned, they headed to the stables, grabbing a coffee from the canteen on the way past. She'd give both the boys a walk in hand and let them pick at some grass before giving them a quick groom and tucking them up in their stables for the night. Sophia and Drop Kick had an early start tomorrow, one of the first into the ring for their show jumping, and then out onto the cross country just before lunch.

Elsa greeted the various grooms working in the barn as she passed them. She loved the social side of being away at events like this; working at home could become so solitary on a small yard like Sophia's.

She put a headcollar on both of the boys and led them out for a quick graze behind the lorry park, returning when she started to feel chilly and wet from the annoying drizzle. She started with Drop Kick first; ran a brush through his mane, curly from his earlier plaits. She wrapped his legs and put a lightweight sheet on him to keep off the late night chill. A sponge over his face and a splash of hoof oil and he was ready for bed.

"How's it going?" the friendly Kiwi groom, Paige, from next door greeted her.

"Yea, not bad." Elsa smiled. "Good dressage?"

"So-so," she smiled. "Looks like we're in for a bit of rain. Are yours real cross country horses?"

"Drop Kick is a machine, but Merlin has low mileage. This weekend is just about getting some good experience for the both of them. All of our horses are having a step up."

"Yea, I heard about you losing Nobby. Bit of a blow."

"Massive blow, but hey," she patted Drop Kick's neck. "Sophia has the chance to prove this weekend that she is not over-reliant on one horse."

"She's a class jockey." Paige agreed.

Elsa nodded. "How do you fancy your chances?"

"Well, Frederick is the one to beat, isn't he? He's on fire."

"Yup, all of his horses are looking fantastic," Elsa reluctantly agreed. "I watched his first dressage – apparently his second was absolutely faultless. Tried his heart out."

"Yea," Paige nodded, smiling. "But boss Brett will give him a run for his money!"

"Good!" Elsa grinned. "Wipe that smug look off his face."

"Hey, smug and arrogant or not, I'm kind of glad he's winning a lot, means we get to watch his gorgeous face splashed across the big screen! Wouldn't kick him out of bed, would you?"

The girls continued to chat and laugh while they skipped out their stalls, and Elsa began to forget about her missed dinner opportunity.

Elsa was up at the crack of dawn the next morning. She led the boys out for a leg stretch before feeding them their breakfast and grooming them until she could almost see her reflection in their coats.

Drop Kick's tack was all lined up; she had oiled the leather work until her arms ached. She hopped aboard Merlin and took him for a quiet hack around the estate, tagging along with a few other competitors who had the same idea. Then she returned him to his stall with a haynet while she readied Drop Kick for the show jumping. By the time she had walked him from the barn, past the lorry park and to the arena on the far side of the estate, he was ready to be worked in. Sophia and Petra waited at the warm up. Elsa adjusted his bridle and gave his studs a final check, oiled his hooves and sponged the foam away from his mouth. She legged Sophia into the saddle, ran a towel around her polished black boots to remove the sticky mud and grass, and went to stand beside the practice jump to await her instructions from Derek as he got the pair warmed up.

Drop Kick left his laziness behind when it came to show jumping. Elsa watched excitedly from the collecting ring as the big gelding hauled Sophia's lithe frame into the ring. He gave a squeal and a buck as they cantered past the judge's box, and received a stern kick from Sophia. Everyone had wondered, when Drop Kick was first purchased, whether he was more of a man's ride and would prove too much for Sophia, but she was not to be defeated and the pair had quickly forged a strong bond.

They bounded through the start and flew over the first, Drop Kick's huge stride eating up the ground as he took on all the fences with ease. Sophia loved show jumping him, and her smile said it all as they flew through the finish with a fast clear.

Elsa was waiting with sugar lumps. She gave the gelding a hearty pat as she took the reins and Sophia slid from the saddle. Elsa loosened his girth and began walking him back to the barn while Sophia went off to discuss the cross-country course with Petra, and get some final tips from Derek.

Elsa untacked Drop Kick and hosed him off. Even though heavy rain had held off for his round, the persistent drizzle had left him soaked, and thick, sticky mud coated his legs and belly. Eventually grey again, Elsa returned him to his stall with a haynet for a rest before he needed to come back out for cross country, and took Merlin out for a leg stretch and a pick of grass. The youngster hated being shut in for too long, and needed stimulation otherwise he set about destroying his stable and walking persistent circles on his white shavings bed until it turned a stodgy, dark brown.

There was time to grab a quick coffee and a bowl of chips from the nearest catering van, and then it was time to get

Drop Kick ready for his much-anticipated cross country round. Elsa had run a wet sponge over his tack before she put it back on him. He wore the same saddle and bridle as for his show jumping round, but she added a padded breastplate to stop his saddle from slipping over the extended distance he would be required to gallop, and all round protective boots, double checking everything to ensure it was fastened correctly. His studs were in, and she gave them a final check with the spanner. The last thing she wanted was him slipping on the increasingly wet course. She applied grease generously to his legs to enable him to slide off the fence were he unfortunate enough to leave a leg.

Sophia appeared in the aisle, hard hat firmly fastened, cross country colours on, her air jacket ready. She keenly tapped her whip against her long leather boots. Drop Kick pawed the ground impatiently; he knew what was coming and he was excited to get on with it.

"Ready?" Elsa smiled.

"You bet!" Sophia beamed, her earlier nerves firmly forgotten.

Elsa legged her into the saddle, threw her rucksack of groom's essentials onto her back, checked that Merlin had sufficient hay and water and accompanied Sophia on the walk to the warm up. Elsa couldn't help but get nervous when horses in her charge set off across country, but the feeling when they crossed the finish line was exhilarating.

Drop Kick gave his customary buck and a delighted squeal as Sophia pushed him into canter, and Elsa couldn't help feeling that today he looked ready; *really* ready to go out there and show everyone just what he was capable of. Sophia popped him over a small brush fence, and he flew it with ease. Elsa couldn't help but smile.

"It's getting wet out there," Elsa heard a returning rider inform his groom as he stripped himself from his body protector. He was absolutely drenched. "Ground is getting really cut up, especially as they watered it, too."

Elsa bit her lip and pulled her coat tighter around her. Drop Kick sure loved a bit of mud to wade through, but she still worried. She stood listening to further feedback as the riders crossed over the finish line and grooms grabbed their horses. It had quickly got wet; *very* wet, but the course was good, however it was proving almost impossible to avoid time penalties.

Frederick was in the start box on his first of three rides in this class. He looked so different to the relaxed, almost smiling person who had asked her to dinner the day before. He looked so focused and in control, like a bomb could go off in front of them and neither he nor his horse would even flinch.

Frederick could afford to be ten seconds over the time and still be in the lead, assuming he otherwise went clear, which was inevitable with the form he was on at the moment. She reluctantly peeled her eyes away.

Sophia was careful not to over warm up Drop Kick. She spent a lot of time with Derek keeping the grey calm and under control. He knew his job so well that he tended to take hold and drag her into fences, and she was quite petite for his huge frame.

She walked him into the start box, and as the starter counted her down, the huge grey launched forward, pulling her out onto the course. Elsa winced as Sophia was hauled from the saddle, taken by surprise as she started her stopwatch, and took a few strides to balance him. They flew the first, Drop Kick giving it inches to spar.

"Oh *God*," Elsa groaned, "he's so fresh."

"This is what happens when you have one top horse to concentrate on," Petra murmured at her side, "the others get forgotten about."

Drop Kick clearly loved his chance to shine. Ears pricked, he hauled Sophia along, and she did well to steer. She gave him a check into a huge table, with an enormous picnic basket decoration, and he seemed to gather his senses and come back to her. He cleared it flawlessly, and Sophia was in perfect control as they strode on into the woodland, and out of Elsa and Petra's view.

"Well, he sure can jump," Petra smiled.

Elsa nodded, and dropped her over loaded rucksack from her straining shoulders as she waited for a glimpse of Sophia on the big screen. They did not have to wait long; the cameras caught her just before the water jump. A small crowd had gathered for this early class, all hoping to see some tumbles into the water throughout the day. Elsa held her breath; hoping that Sophia wouldn't be the first, but Drop Kick splashed happily through the water, kept his footing and jumped cleanly out. Sophia gathered her reins and kicked him on; now that she had him under better control she wasn't afraid to open the throttle and let him run on the long stretches.

She had only four combinations left when she galloped back into Elsa's view, rounding the corner and blasting up the hill towards the finish line. Elsa waited, sweatsheet folded over her arms, ready to throw over Drop Kick's quarters. Drop Kick didn't look like he was lacking any fitness – the only thing that had worried Elsa prior to today's run – and he flew over the huge, wide hay trailer, decorated with a row of bales along the bottom.

She pushed on to the brush fences. They were narrow, and on a dog leg line. Sophia was going for five strides, but Drop Kick pecked on landing of the first element – the ground was so cut up – and threw Sophia off balance. But he was an honest horse and already locked on to the second element. He would never have thought twice about not trying to jump it, but his striding had gone wrong. Sophia kicked on, determined, seeing a long one, but Drop Kick hesitated, got too underneath and then couldn't get enough height as he slid through the mud. He tried to scramble over, but it was too wide. He landed on it, caught his hooves in a tangle and fell off the side, Sophia underneath him.

Elsa gasped, her hand clamped to her mouth. *Get up! Get up! For fuck sake, Sophia, get up!* Frozen to the spot, she watched the close-up on the big screen.

Then Drop Kick got up, and looked around, and wandered off, a leg through his reins but seemingly unharmed. But Sophia lay, motionless.

And then she rolled over, and Elsa let out her breath, and was sprinting down the track to collect her horse, faster than Usain Bolt.

Sophia was rolling around and clutching her shoulder. Two medics bent over her. Someone handed Elsa Drop Kick's reins, and she walked him around and checked him over for injuries. He'd scraped his hock, and a knee, and being grey, the blood made it look worse than it hopefully was. After someone informed her that Sophia needed to get her shoulder checked out, but otherwise seemed alright, Elsa and Drop Kick began the long, lonely walk back to the stables.

Drop Kick's breathing was almost normal by the time they returned to the barn, and his shock seemed to have subsided. Elsa unsaddled him and gave him a bath, checking his cuts weren't too deep as she dried him off, but they seemed to be mostly superficial.

She trotted him up for the vet, who was satisfied he wouldn't need any treatment other than bandaging and cleaning the wounds, and gave him a shot of antibiotics as a precaution.

She had just changed his ice wraps and was holding him outside for a pick of grass when her mobile phone rang. She knew who it would be without even checking the display.

"I've just got to hospital with Sophia." Petra told her. "Are you OK with the horses?"

"Yes, of course. Is she OK?" Elsa asked her anxiously.

"She's better now the painkillers have kicked in, but they want to x-ray her shoulder."

"Oh, bloody hell," Elsa sighed, but she was glad it wasn't any more serious.

"How is Drop Kick?"

"He's fine; just superficial cuts. He might be a bit stiff for a few days but the vet is happy with him."

"Excellent. That's such a relief." She paused. "Are you OK to get packed up and get them both home by yourself?"

She hesitated. "Well, yes, but..."

"Good." Petra cut her off. "I want them both home as soon as possible, before Sophia discharges herself and tries to get back. The stupid bloody mare is convinced she's riding tomorrow, but over my dead body! I might insist on a CT scan while she's in here, to see if she's actually got any brain cells left!"

Elsa laughed. Sophia's determination to ride often clashed with her mother's rationality; it sounded like things were already back to normal.

"Start packing up right now, OK?" Petra instructed sternly. "If the vet is happy Drop Kick is good to travel, get Merlin withdrawn, and hit the road. And if Sophia manages to get hold of you and tells you otherwise, you don't dare listen to her. Understand?"

Elsa nodded. She bit her lip, hoping Petra would take silence for the confirmation she needed.

"Elsa!" she boomed through the phone, and Elsa had to hold it away from her ear. "Do you understand?"

"Yes," Elsa croaked. "I'll get packing right now." She hated lying.

"Good! I'll see you at home. We'll probably be back tomorrow. Have a safe journey; don't leave it too late to set off."

Elsa nodded, and the call was cut.

She went back to the lorry and retrieved Cecil, changed her sodden coat for a dry one, and then it was time to change Drop Kick's ice wraps again.

"Hey, how's the patient?" came the friendly Australian voice over the stall door as she rewrapped Drop Kick's legs.

"He'll be fine," Elsa smiled, standing to meet Ava. "Think he wonders what all the fuss is about."

"I saw it on the big screen," Ava patted his neck. "It was a nasty fall, but he tried so hard to make it. He's very genuine."

"He is," Elsa agreed. "Frustrating, isn't it?"

"That's horses," Ava shrugged, and gave her an encouraging wink. "Happens to the best of us. How is Sophia?"

"Still waiting for an x-ray on her shoulder, but otherwise OK."

"Sounds like she'll be off for a while, then." Ava replied, sympathetic but relieved it wasn't worse. "So, you'll be all on your own tonight?"

"I've got Cecil." Elsa smiled down at her shaggy best friend.

"Well, head on over to our lorry if you and Cecil run out of conversation. I'll have the Barbie going, and a few of the other grooms are coming over, in-between changing leg wraps and stuff – you know how it is."

"A Barbie?" Elsa laughed. "Have you seen the weather?"

"I'm an Aussie!" Ava laughed. "I never go eventing without my Barbie! Plus, Frederick keeps the wine fridge well stocked." she winked. "What more persuasion do you need?"

"I'm not sure wine with Frederick is my idea of relaxing after a stressful day," Elsa replied, eyebrows raised.

"Ah, he won't drink it with us," Ava laughed, "he gets his head down early when we're away at events. He's very...*focused*. Plus, he doesn't like being ogled by sober grooms, let alone drunk ones!"

Elsa smiled. While it did sound tempting; sipping undoubtedly expensive wine in the comfort of Frederick

Twemlow's plush lorry awning with some enjoyable company, after today's drama, all she wanted to do was get her head down and have a little cry at how shit Napier had turned out for them.

Elsa was hand grazing Merlin behind the stable block, when her mobile phone started ringing. Cecil had gone after a rabbit in the undergrowth and was yet to resurface. Elsa pulled the phone from her pocket and stared at the display – a landline she didn't recognise – and hit the answer button with a sense of knowing.

"Hey!" Sophia gasped. "I was really worried you wouldn't answer!"

"I had a feeling it would be you," Elsa smiled. "How are you feeling?"

"High on painkillers. How's my boy?" she asked anxiously.

"Drop Kick is going to be fine," Elsa replied. "He's virtually unscathed and happy as Larry, enjoying everyone fussing over him."

"I'm *so* pleased," Sophia breathed a sigh of relief. "Mum said he was OK, but I couldn't be sure until I asked you myself. Are you still at Napier?"

"Yes," Elsa replied cautiously. "I was slowly packing up, at Petra's instruction..."

"Don't you dare!" Sophia cut her off. "She's such a cheeky mare!"

Elsa laughed. "Funny, she says the same about you!"

"My mobile is still in the lorry, so I couldn't call you! Do you know how long it's taken me to figure out how to use this payphone? And that was only after I'd scrounged some change off some guy!"

Elsa couldn't stop laughing; she was so happy that Sophia really was OK. Merlin cropped gratefully at the grass, his ears flicking back and forth as he listened.

"Don't you dare take the boys home. I think I'm in a hotel

tonight, I'm all strapped up and they're letting me out soon. I'll be back in the morning, and I'm riding if it kills me."

"Your mum will kill you, and me." Elsa replied, nervously chewing her lip.

"Leave her to me. There is absolutely *no* way I'm withdrawing Merlin. I'm not letting Rosie down, she's been so excited about this weekend."

Elsa pulled her coat tighter around her as the drizzle refused to subside. Nobody could find fault with Sophia's loyalty to those who supported her.

"You'd better be on best behaviour tomorrow," she told Merlin, gently tugging on his ear. "Your mum is going to need all the help she can get."

Chapter Four

Elsa was exhausted by the time she returned to the lorry. She peeled off her wet clothes and left them in a heap by the door. What was supposed to have been a warm, fun, come-back weekend had turned into a wet and miserable crock of shit.

She pulled her warm, cosy, ever-so-unflattering tracksuit on, and gathered Cecil up in her arms. Cecil lived for rain and mud, and he'd certainly made the most of it this weekend, for he well and truly stank.

"You need a bath, boy," she told him, giving him a kiss nonetheless. She would make sure he was under the hose tomorrow when she bathed Merlin.

She sighed. She hoped Sophia knew what she was doing, and wasn't at too much risk of doing herself even more damage. There was always another day, but there was no point in trying to tell Sophia that. If she had it in her head that she was going to compete; then Merlin had better be ready, because he *would* be jumping.

Elsa pulled open the fridge door to be greeted by half a bottle of sparkling water and a leftover sandwich courtesy of Petra. Her wet, hungry, cold soul yearned for something hot. She had been meaning to get something from the canteen all day, but it was too late now; there was no way she was going out again. Petra's sandwich would have to do.

Cecil whined and licked his lips as Elsa removed the soggy bread from its Clingfilm. Not too reluctantly she tossed him half and he snapped it eagerly from the air.

"That barely even touched the sides," she ruffled his shaggy hair. "Anyone would think you never get fed."

He licked his lips and curled up in his bed, content. Elsa glared exhaustedly at the filthy leatherwork she had surrounded herself with, and the large bowl of soapy warm water. Drop Kick's tack had accumulated quite a lot of mud on the way around the course. It had to be cleaned off at some point, and Elsa considered there was no time like the presence, especially if bits of it needed to be sparkling and ready for Merlin tomorrow, in case he needed any last-minute emergency replacements. Sophia's horses weren't blessed with endless sets of tack. It looked like her lonely night really would be filled with cleaning grotty, mud-covered, wet, smelly tack.

Cecil's head shot up, and he immediately spun to the door. He barked, and Elsa waited. A sharp knock sounded, and Elsa frowned. She was reluctant to get up, but she knew she must.

She swung the door open, restrained her hound, and let her eyes adjust to the dark. And then she gasped. Frederick stood before her, in all his beauty; a thick mop of tousled blonde curls. He looked so casual. Elsa thought she were going to faint. Why the *fuck* hadn't she showered and at least dressed properly?

Cecil was snarling. His hackles were raised as he made sure Frederick saw his sharp teeth.

Frederick had barely noticed her, his eyes were fixated on Cecil, aghast. "Good *God*! What on earth is that?" he looked the snarling, shaggy mutt up and down.

"*He* is called Cecil," Elsa replied haughtily, eventually finding her voice. "And *he* is the only man I have room for in my life. Apart from Nobby, but you already took him."

Oh, she cringed. What on earth made her think he was here for her? What if he'd come to tell her one of Sophia's horses had developed colic or something else serious, and she'd just been rude to him?

And then he looked at her, for the first time since he'd knocked on her door. He took in every inch of her, his beautiful blue eyes slowly roaming her appreciatively from head to toe, and back up. His eyes stopped on hers, and she felt her heart quicken. He looked divine. As she towered over him from up on the lorry she couldn't help but think how different he looked to when he was high up on a huge warmblood, exuding power, superiority and arrogance. He suddenly looked so vulnerable, and *shy*. She could almost believe he looked normal, were he not so abnormally good looking.

"I thought you'd be lonely." He murmured softly, knowing immediately he'd made the right decision to finally pluck up the courage to knock on her lorry.

She jumped in surprise. She just stood there, speechless. "Well, I'm not." She shrugged eventually.

"So I see." He smiled, nervously regarding Cecil who had at least stopped snarling. "Can I come in anyway? My lorry appears to have been taken over by everyone else's grooms...*again*." He gave a dramatic roll of his eyes, but Elsa decided he didn't really look too bothered about it, and he waited expectantly

Unable to think of a plausible reason why not, apart from that she must look like she'd been dragged through a hedge and that her lorry stank, Elsa reluctantly stepped aside and he climbed up.

"Good *God*," he hesitated in the doorway, his face screwed up in disgust. "What is that *smell*?"

The door to the horse area was closed and Elsa had swept it out as soon as they'd arrived. But even she couldn't deny the stench that filled the living area.

"You mean wet, filthy dog mixed with equally wet, muddy, sweaty leather?" she asked from below raised eyebrows. "That's my favourite aroma."

He regarded her suspiciously. He had a crisp blue shirt on, cream chinos and brown shoes, and held a carrier bag, and oh *God* he smelled *heavenly*. She didn't quite know what to do when someone *that* good looking was standing in front of her, when she was looking *like this*.

"You'll have to excuse the mess. I'm cleaning tack." She said feebly, her cheeks flushed.

"Very commendable." He smiled. "Your employer will be pleased."

"I don't think she is all too pleased at the moment."

"Yes, you're right." He immediately looked regretful. "Thoughtless of me. Is she OK?"

"Bit bruised" Elsa shrugged. "Buggered shoulder, but apart from that she'll be fine."

"Good. So, you're alone tonight?" He held up the bag. "I brought wine. One of each. I wasn't sure which you prefer." He paused. "And food – do you like Chinese?"

She tried to restrain herself. Her stomach begged her to be filled with Chinese right now, and the aroma was already filling the lorry. She narrowed her eyes at him. "What's the catch?"

Cecil barked at him, his hackles and teeth refusing to subside.

"He doesn't appear to be very keen on me." Frederick acknowledged nervously.

"I am cautious of people who he doesn't like." Elsa told him coldly, her arms folded defensively across her chest. "His instincts are usually much better than mine."

He looked shy, awkward even. "Elsa," he began quietly, "we somehow appear to have got off on the wrong foot. You seem to have some warped perception of me, and I'd like to put that right."

She felt herself blushing. He was such a smooth talker. Was she really as cold to him on the outside, as she felt on the inside? And he had noticed, but did he actually care?

"I'm surprised you even noticed." She murmured quietly.

"I notice a lot of things, Elsa, but I only act on the most important."

"And me being cold towards you is important?"

He held her gaze. His gorgeous bright blue eyes searched

hers and she felt herself shrinking. *How did he do that?*

"Yes," he whispered. "Very."

Oh God. She suddenly wanted to kiss him so bad. She didn't need this; beautiful, kissable strangers letting themselves into her lorry and distracting her from her work. *With wine and food.*

"Let me help you clean that leather," he murmured, as if reading her mind.

"You know how to clean tack?" she asked him, eyebrows arched.

"I think you'd be surprised at the hard graft that I can put in," he told her quietly. "But there's no need for you to go telling my staff about my hidden talents. I don't want them getting any ideas."

She giggled, and he caught his breath and stared at her in admiration.

"You have a lovely laugh," he told her quietly.

She felt herself blushing further and quickly looked away, desperate to change her focus onto anything but his soft eyes and totally kissable lips.

"But I'm not so sure about the dress sense," he teased, as he studied her with a smile.

"You can sit down," she murmured helplessly, forcing herself to turn away and pointing at the sofa covered in saddles. She quickly moved them, trying to hide her own smile and wishing he'd stop watching her; it put her on edge.

"Sorry about the hairs," she mumbled.

"It's OK; I can cope with the hair. Part of the job," he told her, amusement twinkling in those soft, blue eyes. "Gets everywhere, doesn't it?"

She nodded. But he didn't sit.

"It's surprising how much room is in these little lorries," he looked around himself.

Elsa imagined the luxury of his own lorry, and felt a stab of jealously. "I'm afraid this one doesn't come equipped with wine glasses." She told him sharply.

"That's OK," he smiled easily. "We can swig from the bottle."

She gawped at him. *We?* Was he seriously intending on staying?

"I do like the attire, by the way," he winked. "Weren't you planning on going out again this evening?"

She felt her cheeks flaming. Cecil had stopped barking, as confused by the stranger's presence as she was, but never taking his eyes from him.

"I'm teasing you," he smiled. "Can my food and I stay, or are you sending us away?"

"*You,*" she prodded him lightly in the chest, and jumped at how solid it was. "Can do what the hell you like, but the food and wine stays."

"Then I shall stay. Do you have plates?"

"Don't push it. If you're lucky I might have a fork, but we'll probably have to share."

"That's fine by me." He replied huskily, and she felt her heart lurch. "You have what you like, I'm not so hungry. But pass me the cloth if you want me to work."

She frowned and did as he said. He perched on the end of the seat, that she hadn't seen the point of rearranging into her bed yet if Sophia was not returning tonight, and scrubbed at the filthy leather. She pulled her duvet around her shoulders, and watched him for a moment, trying to make sense of it all in her head as she devoured hungry mouthfuls of sweet, divine Chinese and swigged from the wine bottle.

Frederick Twemlow sat in her lorry, just she and him, scrubbing at her leather work. No one would ever believe her, were she to tell them. But she wouldn't be telling anyone.

"Did you always want to be a groom?" he looked up, disturbing her from her thoughts, as he wiped the sponge over the stirrup leathers.

She shrugged and passed him the wine bottle. "I suppose

so."

He took a swig and passed it back. "Did you never want to ride?"

"Maybe, at the very beginning. But I'm better suited to this." She didn't want to tell him about Bear – how the little mare had rekindled her own love for nice, smooth paces and flying over fences – or where she saw the pair of them in the future. Her dreams were massive for her, but would look so lowly compared to Frederick's own impressive achievements.

"Do you always want to be a groom?"

"Are you going to question me all night?" she demanded.

His head shot up and his hand stilled. "So, I can stay all night?" he smiled.

He looked hopeful. His question caught her off guard and she felt herself blushing – again. Geez what was wrong with her? She was behaving like a teenager. Did she want him to stay all night? What girl in her right mind wouldn't?

"If you've come looking for a one-night-stand, then you're not going to find one here," she told him coldly.

"You think that's what I want?" his eyebrows rose.

"I've absolutely no idea what you want," she shrugged. "But that would be my first guess."

"I'm hurt that you'd even think that of me," he told her with a small smile. "I won't even touch you, I promise."

"I'm not sure you'd be able to put up with Cecil's snoring," she told him. She picked up the TV remote to distract herself, give herself some time. Her hands were shaking as she flicked through the TV's limited, crackly channels.

"Where do you sleep?" he looked around, as if looking for another bedroom.

"Well, Mister, there's no pop out sides or other luxuries to this lorry," she replied, amused. "Sophia normally sleeps above the cab, and I put the table down and sleep down here with Cecil."

"I see," he smiled.

"But tonight, Sophia's not here, so I might as well jump in the Luton." She put her empty plate in the sink. She would wash up tomorrow; she was far too tired to worry about that now, and snuggled back into her duvet. She tried not to look at him as he lingered by the door, putting back together the leather pieces of the bridles and martingales he had so meticulously cleaned.

So, Sophia wouldn't be back all night. He tried to hide his joy at this welcome news, a flicker of guilt for his fellow rider still laying in hospital. With his large number of rides, he knew that statistically he had more chance of winding up in hospital than most – eventing was like that. It might just as easy be him hitting the deck next week and being fed through a straw. *So, I might as well make the most of the time that I'm not,* he thought.

"Would you like me to stay?" he asked quietly. "Because I'm a big boy now, I can take being told to shove off."

She hesitated. She couldn't imagine anyone had ever told him to shove off. "I'm not sure it would be humane of me to send you back to a lorry-load of drunk grooms," she evened. "God knows what they might do to you."

"I am rather defenceless and feeble," he reasoned, nodding.

"Feel free to stay," she heard herself saying, "but I need an early night."

He grinned like a cat that had got the cream. She tried to ignore the pretty-boy smile, her head in turmoil with her own emotions. *What the hell was she playing at?*

"It's a bit chilly in here, isn't it," he frowned.

"Do you wish to be derogatory about my living arrangements, any further?" she glared at him.

"I do not, I apologise." He still smiled. "But please may I share some of your duvet?"

She wanted to giggle. His smile was infectious. *Please may I share?* How old were they, seriously? He was so posh. She opened her arm up and he snuggled inside. She gasped as he brushed against her; her senses were on fire.

"You won't even know I'm here." He told her huskily.

Elsa wasn't so sure about that. How on earth could she not be affected by the dazzling body beside her?

Elsa had never had such a hard time trying to get to sleep before. It had been an overly long, stressful day and she didn't think she'd ever felt so tired, yet the warmth of his body beside her prevented sleep from coming. He made her senses feel so wakened and alive. She couldn't remember the last time she'd been in such close proximity to a *boy*, and it had never been such a good looking one. He was fully clothed, yet just the thought of what deliciousness lay underneath that shirt kept her heart beating fast.

And *Oh. My. God.* She wanted to touch him. She really, *really* wanted to touch him and run her hands over that divine body of his, but she didn't want the consequences of what that could lead to. She'd just be another notch on his bedpost. He'd probably never speak to her again, she'd feel dirty and used, and it would add to the Nobby fiasco. She reminded herself sternly, that she despised this man for what he'd done to Sophia, their yard, and their team.

But she'd warmed to him tonight. She was surprised at herself how easily she had let it happen. He didn't seem quite so arrogant as she'd let herself believe. She remembered Ava's words, about him being so focused. Yet here he was, the night before the all-important show jumping – in the lead of the main *big* class after cross country – sleeping in such close proximity to her. In Sophia's small lorry, she could almost *touch him*. In fact, save for their clothes, parts of her were already touching him, and her senses were on fire.

Maybe if she made it through the night without touching him, and he without her, she'd know he truly was a gentleman and definitely worth another look. And if he couldn't get what he wanted and lost interest, well, no loss. After all, you couldn't miss what you hadn't had, could you?

He must have come here looking to score. Oh, he'd be *so* disappointed in her, she thought with glee, if only she could keep up her resist of temptation.

She watched him sleep. A wisp of blond hair fell across his forehead, stopped just above his closed eyes. She desperately wanted to brush it away from those perfect thick eyelashes that curled skywards, and were the envy of any girl.

"No touching," he whispered, making her jump as an eye sprung open.

"I wasn't going to," she lied, blushing. "I was just watching."

There was a moment's silence. From the floor, Cecil snored, finally reluctantly at rest with this intruder in his lorry.

"I am sorry, about the horse, you know?" Frederick said, closing his eye again. "I didn't know it would mean so much to you."

"Because one horse could never mean much to you?" she asked bitterly.

"Please, Elsa." He sighed. "I thought we were getting somewhere."

"Why did you text me?" she asked a moment later. The reason behind his strange, lying text still niggled at her.

"I was worried about him." Frederick murmured hesitantly.

"Bollocks!" she replied, indignant.

"Get some sleep, Elsa," he told her gently. "We've both got a busy day tomorrow."

She subconsciously wondered whether he still might take any clothes off. She really hoped he might, yet also helplessly hoped that he wouldn't. She really did envision the marvels of the body that lay under that shirt; it was bound to be as fantastic as the rest of him. She wanted to see it, but if she saw it then she'd without doubt have to touch it. And where did this all end? Most likely in tears, she thought, briefly desolate.

She folded her arms defiantly across her chest, determined she was not even going to accidentally touch him.

His clothes stayed on, and she breathed relief and disappointment both in the same breath. She knew she could not move all night; she was tense as she tried to remain rock still. You could have heard a pin drop in the silence between them, but all Elsa could hear was the loud beating of her heart in her eardrums. She felt certain it was loud enough for him to hear it, too.

His eyes were closed. His arrogance was gone and he suddenly looked so vulnerable. Elsa felt that she could happily watch him all night.

At some point during the night, Elsa did manage to succumb to sleep, she realised as she awoke to Frederick silently trying to leave without disturbing her. She frowned as he tucked the duvet back around her, and did not seem concerned when she opened her eye to him.

"Sorry, I was trying not to wake you," he whispered. "I wasn't sure when you had to be up. But I'm not sure your hound will let me out unscathed."

"He's sure got my back," she smiled. Cecil was being patiently quiet, but his teeth were threatening to come out, and although his growl was remaining barely audible, it was definitely there.

Frederick brushed her loose hair from her face, and she flinched at his soft touch. He trailed a slender index finger slowly across her cheek, letting it linger longer than was necessary, and for the first time she really wished he wouldn't go.

"Busy day today," he smiled gently, as if reading her mind. "Thank you for providing me with refuge last night."

"Any time," she found herself saying, and immediately cursed herself. She blamed it on her sleep-deprived state. "I'm sure you can look after yourself, though," she added quickly. "I'm sure you're used to females hounding you."

"You'd be surprised," he whispered, and stood up, her skin going cold where he had touched her. "I'll see you soon."

She nodded, suddenly hopeful that he meant it, and it not just being one of those things you automatically said to someone when really you had no intention of ever seeing them again.

"Good luck today," she called after him as he let himself out.

"Thank you," he smiled – a genuine, heartfelt smile, and paused halfway down the lorry steps. "And please send my best wishes to Sophia."

She nodded, but of course she couldn't do that – how on earth would she ever explain this one? She was not even sure she understood it herself.

The door was closed and he was gone. She wondered what had they just shared? She pulled the duvet up to her face and took a deep breath of the glorious scent he had left behind, and wished she could stay in this happy cocoon forever. But at this unearthly time of morning when most of her non-horsey friends' back home were rolling in from their night out, Elsa was reluctantly dragging herself up from her bed. Her horses needed her, and today was likely going to be both stressful and busy.

The lorry door firmly closed behind him, Frederick took a deep breath as he ran his hands down his face. He needed a moment to gather his thoughts before returning to his own lorry and normality. For the first time in his adult life he had spent the night sleeping beside a beautiful woman and not touched her. And he had wanted to, alright. He had wanted to run his hands all over her, through her gorgeous caramel hair, and kiss those soft lips. He could only imagine how sweet they tasted. It had been so tough for him not to do any of those things, and he was having trouble understanding why he hadn't.

Despite his sleepless night, he felt more awake than ever. He walked quickly to his lorry, trying to salvage his focus on the show jumping that lay ahead. But his mind kept wandering back to the pretty little lady he'd left sleeping in her bed. He was proud of himself for not touching her, but it had done nothing to quash his desire of wanting to.

Chapter Five

Elsa removed Drop Kick's leg wraps and was pleased to feel that his legs were not hot, and only a little puffy from where he had been standing.

He had a few bumps and scratches, and was undeniably stiff, but as she walked him around the lorry park he loosened up and the puffiness around his tendons subsided. His ears were forward and he was already back to his perky, cheeky self, and Elsa was so pleased. She felt a great sense of relief. She gave him a hearty pat as she returned him to his stall, and he greedily tucked into his breakfast.

"Fancy a hack?" Ava called over the stall door, as Elsa brushed Merlin off.

"Sure," Elsa smiled, Merlin's tack already slung ready over the stall door.

They quickly saddled up and headed out around the back of the stable block, away from the trade stands and the people, the displays and the rings. The huge estate was quiet, so pretty and peaceful once away from the hustle and bustle.

"Didn't fancy a glass of vino last night, then?" Ava probed.

"I did, but -" she broke off, hesitant. "It was a long day, sorry. Sleep got the better of me."

"That's OK, I won't hold it against you." She smiled. "Freddy will be on one today; he didn't come out of his room once last night, and he was up and out before me this morning."

Elsa nodded, pretending she wasn't in the least bit interested. But while trying to fall asleep, Elsa's biggest fear had been waking up and finding him gone, and that had almost happened. She wondered whether he had wanted to say goodbye, whether he wanted to see her again. *What on earth did he want from her?* Her heart swelled as she tried impossibly to put him firmly to the back of her mind, and concentrate on what she was really here for.

The conversation quickly turned to the starting order for the day, how they thought each competitor would fare, and who would come out on top. As far as Ava was concerned – and secretly Elsa – Frederick had the title in the bag, but this was a horse trials, destined to test both horse and rider to the maximum, and anything could happen, despite only having one phase of the competition left.

They deliberated how Sophia would fare, both sharing their concerns for her health and safety, and then they turned onto the track through the endless acres of woodland, and shortened their reins for a canter, and the wind in their face dissolved all of their deliberations.

Rosie stood peering over Merlin's stable door, her eyes wide and her face as white as a sheet.

"Are you *sure* it's a good idea?" she implored, as Elsa brushed the gelding's dusty saddle marks away. "I mean, he's enough of a handful when you have fully functioning limbs!"

"I know," Elsa anxiously bit her lip, but didn't stop brushing. "But Sophia knows what she's doing." At least, she really hoped that she did.

"Oh, I know, but I don't want her injuring herself further on my account! I really don't mind if she withdraws – there will be other events." Rosie sighed, running a hand through her immaculate hair. "I told her that on the phone, but you know what she's like!"

Elsa nodded.

"Can't you say something to her?" Rosie asked quietly, after a moment's thought. "She listens to you, she *trusts* you."

"Oh no, *no*," Elsa insisted fearfully, wishing for this conversation to be over. "I'm *just* the groom. My responsibility is the horses."

"Oh *God*, my nerves can't cope with this," another hand ran through Rosie's hair. "I need a drink!" She turned. "I'll be in the member's marquee!" she called over her shoulder, as she scurried off down the aisle.

Elsa was running a brush over Drop Kick's sleek coat, when she heard the well wishes call out into the aisle from various grooms, riders and owners, and she let out a sigh of relief at Sophia's arrival. Her shoulder was strapped up, her arm raised and pinned against her chest in a sling, and Elsa wondered with some trepidation how on earth she was going to guide a young, green horse around a bold, testing cross country course. That was if she even made it through the dressage and show jumping beforehand.

"Hope you weren't too lonely without me?" Sophia beamed over Drop Kick's door.

"Surprisingly not," Elsa replied, not wishing to elaborate and hiding her guilt well as she crouched to adjust his leg wraps. "How are you feeling?"

"Determined," Sophia told her, not giving much away. She observed Elsa in silence, but Elsa wished she'd talk.

She needed to get Frederick Twemlow off her mind, but that was seemingly impossible this morning. But she couldn't tell Sophia about it, even though nothing had happened. She hated to admit it, but she'd wanted it to. She wished he'd touched her. She was so frustrated that he hadn't; she'd had no time for dating since she'd come to work for Sophia. Her last relationship had just fizzled out as horses took up too much of her time, and they hadn't been that into each other anyway – neither had been willing to put in much effort to make it work.

Any kind of attention would have been nice recently, but she hadn't expected it to come from the best-looking guy on the eventing circuit. *The one who had stolen their best horse*, she reminded herself bitterly.

She often thought it would be nice to share things with

someone; someone to come home to, someone to chat to, but how would she fit them in when she spent all hours out on the yard, and the weekends at competitions? That was why Cecil was so important to her.

"Didn't go hang out with any of the other grooms or riders?" Sophia asked, breaking her from her thoughts.

"I was shattered," Elsa replied, and that bit wasn't a lie. "Drop Kick was fine but I still had to keep checking on him, you know – I didn't get much sleep."

Sophia nodded. "Of course, sorry. I was so bored in the hotel room. I kept telling Mum not to be silly and take me back to the lorry, but she was adamant you'd already taken the horses' home, and we'd be best to tackle the journey after a decent night's sleep."

"Very wise," Elsa smiled. She could just imagine the look on Sophia's face if she'd returned to her lorry to find her groom in bed with Frederick Twemlow – innocent and fully clothed or not.

"Not so wise when I told her this morning you were still here. She was shooting daggers at me the whole journey back. Nearly drove us off the road twice."

"You'll be getting me sacked," Elsa laughed.

"I'm sure someone else will have you," Sophia told her with a wink. "Especially if you keep turning my horses out so immaculately!"

The horses' tack was shining from its midnight clean, and Elsa had laid out everything Merlin would need, in order. Elsa put him on the lunge line behind the stabling, and watched with a heavy heart as he proceeded to squeal and buck, and kick up the turf. There was no way Sophia was going to be getting on him any time soon, so Elsa was glad she had had the sense to get him ready extra early. Hopefully by the time his slot came around he'd be so bored and half asleep.

Sophia looked on, her shoulder heavily strapped under her

coat. Luckily nothing was broken, but Elsa could tell she was in more pain than she cared to let on. Petra stood by her daughter's side, still looking as furious as when she had first arrived, and Elsa was glad she mainly worked with the horses, not people.

"He was fine when I hacked him this morning," Elsa shrugged. She pulled him to a halt and ran his stirrups down the leathers.

"Don't you dare!" Petra roared, when she saw her daughter prepare to move. "Elsa will work him in."

Elsa nodded and pulled her hard hat on, and Petra legged her into the saddle.

The walk to the warm up ring avoiding the small crowds was long and pleasant, taking her along the edge of the woodland and the open grazing fields of this vast estate. Merlin plodded along content, and she gradually shortened his reins and asked him to listen to her. He was so soft and obliging for such a green horse, and her earlier fears for Sophia slowly evaporated. She pushed him into a trot, alternating between pushing him out beneath her in long, ground-covering strides, to shortening up and bringing him back to her. She brought him back to a walk as they approached the warm-up, and allowed him to take in the hustle and bustle of the sights before him.

Elsa took a deep breath. While she was always schooling and hacking Sophia's horses at home, she normally only jumped on them at shows to loosen them up, cool them off or hack them around the showground for some downtime. Never did she mingle with the big names in the warm-up.

"Please don't chuck me," she whispered nervously to Merlin, gently pulling on his ear. "Please don't show me up, or my name will be mud!"

She worked him in without fault until Sophia arrived, her pristine white breeches and tight, black dressage jacket telling Elsa she was ready. Her sling was gone, freeing her injured arm, but she held it awkwardly and Elsa doubted how much use it would be to her. She winced as Petra legged her up into the saddle, and desperately tried to hide her discomfort.

"I'm just going to go for a walk first," she said, her brave face firmly on. "As long as he doesn't pull too much and I only have to steer, I'll be fine."

"He's been as soft as butter," Elsa reassured her.

"At least the rain has held off today," Sophia smiled. "And I get to go early; the ground is holding up nicely."

She walked Merlin around the outside of the warm up, and ambled along the back of the trade stands, close to a section of the cross-country course where a galloping pair were just coming out of the woodland and down the hill to the next obstacle. Elsa was glad she had walked Merlin around here several times since arriving, so that he now really was accustomed to his surroundings and found little reason to spook.

If there was one horse Elsa trusted to look after an injured rider, it was Merlin. Although young, he was genuine and honest, and it was as if he sensed that *her up there* would need a little extra help today, and it really was time for him to pack in the silliness and don his big boy shoes.

Sophia gave Elsa a nod to tell her all was OK, and she took Merlin into the warm up, and quickly put the already well worked in gelding through his paces. And then she was up next, and the steward called her into the collecting ring. Merlin was halted while Elsa ran a sponge across his face, wiped the foam from his mouth, and splashed hoof oil on his wet hooves, and the pair were good to go.

Sophia pushed him into a trot and they entered the ring, and Elsa couldn't remember ever being this nervous watching a dressage test before. She knew that as a young horse, Merlin needed his rider to give him their all and to fill him with confidence. He could not be relied upon to get himself out of trouble, but she had faith that Sophia would not have clamoured into the saddle if she'd thought at any point she'd let him down. Rosie stood behind her, snatching anxious glances of his test from behind her generously filled, large wine glass.

Merlin behaved impeccably for a horse of his inexperience. There were a few sticky moments, an over-excited trot that Sophia struggled to contain, and some miscommunications when she simply hadn't the strength to half halt or ask for more bend, and instead he impersonated a giraffe. Some of the circles looked a bit crooked, but the overall performance and even the score were promising.

He left the ring on a long rein, with adoring pats from Sophia, and Elsa waited with sugar lumps. Sophia slid from the saddle, all smiles, and Elsa took the reins and loosened his girths.

"How are you feeling?" Petra questioned.

"Great!" Sophia replied honestly. "He was a *darling*."

"Are you sure you can take him across country though?" Petra demanded, concerned. "It's a big course, and he's very young. He will need your help."

"Well, we'll see how the show jumping goes," Sophia shrugged. "If I manage to not get myself eliminated then I don't see why not."

Petra shook her head in despair. "I hope when you have children they give you as much grief as you do me."

Elsa lead Merlin away, trying to contain her smiles. There was time for him to nibble a haynet and tell Drop Kick all about his dressage before he had to come back out again.

The main cross country course was beginning to draw the crowds now, as the big names began to head out in the main class. The Kiwi's were on top form in the big classes, and Brett stormed into the top ten, with only a couple of time faults to add to his already impressive dressage score. Elsa was pleased; she'd have something positive to chat to Paige about back at the barn, after all.

The rain was still holding off when Elsa brought the gelding back out for show jumping. She worked him in and checked his studs one last time before legging Sophia up. She popped him over a small practice jump, and Elsa noticed she was anxiously chewing her bottom lip as she cantered past them at the side rail. Elsa hugged the sweatsheet closer to her chest. She just wished that people like Christine Forrester could see the guts that Sophia was currently displaying, her determination not to give up, and what she put herself through for her horses, her sport and her supporters, when really, she should be tucked up in bed, resting. But they wouldn't care.

Merlin behaved impeccably, and Sophia really did only have to steer him around the forgiving course, for just eight faults when she had got him in too close to an oxer, and had the last pole of the treble. But Sophia simply hadn't the strength to give him the required pull, and Elsa knew she'd be annoyed at herself for that. Elsa was so proud of him, and was waiting with sugar cubes as soon as he left the ring. Sophia threw her arm around him.

"Excuse me," a steward interrupted. "Would you mind heading over for your presentation now?"

"Presentation?" Both Elsa and Sophia queried in unison. The competition was not over yet and there was no way Sophia would be in contention for a place anyway, with rails down in the show jumping.

"Yes," the steward smiled, double checking the clip board she held. "Number thirty-seven, Sophia Hamilton and Magic Merlin. Your groom is Elsa Aldridge?" she looked to Elsa for confirmation.

Slowly, Elsa nodded. She was not used to being noticed at events, especially not on full name terms; she spent her time blending in behind the scenes.

"Our panel have chosen Magic Merlin as the best turned out horse over the whole horse trials," the steward beamed.

Elsa stared at her, certain she must have misheard. "I've won the best turned out?"

"You sure have! Would you like to come over – Lady Amelia is ready to present you with the Henry Turnbridge cup?"

Elsa felt her eyes welling up. The Henry Turnbridge cup was a big deal at Napier – all the grooms wanted to seize it. The best turned out prize was sponsored generously by the late Henry's family – an avid eventer who had been cruelly taken too young after a fatal fall out on course. The Turnbridge's were determined to do something positive in Henry's memory; while the reminder was always there how dangerous their sport was. Elsa had never in a million years believed the coveted trophy could ever possibly be hers.

Sophia's arm was around her shoulder. "You go and get your trophy," she whispered down into her ear. "You deserve this."

The eager steward was already ushering her forward towards the secretary's marquee. There was a table where all the trophies and rosettes were laid out for each class. A beautiful, blonde lady looking immaculate in a daring orange suit, stepped forward and eagerly shook Elsa's hand at the steward's announcement that the winner of the best turned out was here.

"Lady Amelia *Twemlow*," the immaculate lady purred. "Such a pleasure to meet you."

Twemlow, Elsa felt her heart slow. Of course, Frederick's mother. All the similarities were there, and it was not difficult to see where Frederick inherited his looks from. His mother was beautiful; not a strand of hair was out of place, large pearls graced her ears. Her hands were so soft, Elsa noticed, like she had never attempted a day's work in her life.

"Lovely to meet you, too," Elsa croaked, clearing her voice and determined not to feel intimidated.

"Your horse looked stunning," Lady Amelia affirmed. "A real credit to you." She was passed the silver Henry

Turnbridge cup, and she held it out to Elsa so that the small crowd gathered around them could take their photo. "I am delighted to present to you, on behalf of the Turnbridge family, the Henry Turnbridge cup."

Elsa could barely focus; it felt surreal. *Mrs Twemlow,* the voices in her head declared, *your son spent last night in my lorry – what does he want from me?* But instead Lady Amelia was giving a speech to the small gathering of equestrian magazine reporters, shaking Elsa's hand and then thrusting her towards them. All that Elsa could manage to say was how shocked yet honoured she was to receive this award.

"Sophia Hamilton," the reporter beamed at Sophia. "Magic Merlin was looking fantastic, as do all of your horses, which was why you stood out to our panel. What does it mean to you to have someone like Elsa in your team?"

Elsa felt as though her heart was going to burst with pride.

There was not time to head back to the barn before cross country, and the rain was starting to fall. Elsa cursed as she pulled her hard hat on and jumped on, walking Merlin around so that Sophia could stay out of the rain. Was it really too much to ask that her one-armed jockey at least got a dry run across country to finish the day on?

Merlin jogged sideways and lowered his head in aversion when she asked him to walk into the rain, but she nudged him on and told him to get on with it. He was getting excited now; he knew exactly what fun came after the show jumping, and he couldn't wait to get on with it. She remembered when she'd first come to work at Sophia's, her first job out of school, and the next step up from tacking up the ponies at the local riding school on her weekends, and taking her aged pony to pony club rallies. She'd been amazed by the sheer size of the eventers, thought they needed special treatment and wrapping up in cotton wool. But they were just horses; just like those at the riding school. She didn't treat them any different, but she had learned so much from both Sophia and all the horses that had passed through her yard. She no longer felt so inferior among the other, more experienced grooms, and now she had the trophy to show that she could mingle with the best of them.

Sophia appeared after Elsa had put Merlin through a canter on both reins, and Elsa legged her up into the saddle to let them get sufficiently worked in before they went to the start.

Derek appeared, ready to put her through her paces. In Merlin's younger days, he had really lacked confidence, and Sophia really had to ride him into fences to prevent him backing off, but with increased outings she had found herself gradually using less energy and enjoying the ride a lot more.

Elsa waited nervously at the rail, barely able to watch. This was going to be a massive test for the pair of them even before Sophia's accident; she really hoped Sophia was doing the right thing. But she was not one to be argued with.

She subconsciously looked around for Frederick, but he was nowhere to be seen. The crowds of female fans gathering normally announced his presence, but there was barely anyone for these smaller classes. Most of them had already tackled the cross-country course for the big class – a class Sophia would have duly attended had Nobby still been with them – and were waiting for the show jumping finale.

Elsa gave Merlin's girth a final check and Sophia was called into the start box. The starter counted her down, she pressed her watch, and she was off. Elsa was ringing her palms, hopping from foot to foot, unable to stay still.

The first few fences were easy, designed not to be too challenging for these young horses, but to help get them settled and into a rhythm. But they were not easy to an almost one-armed jockey, and Elsa rode every fence with her. Merlin quickly settled down, and took them in his stride. Elsa didn't realise she'd been holding her breath, until he was over the fifth and disappeared down the hill, and out of her sight. She could only wait until he appeared the other side of the woodland.

She took a deep breath and looked to Petra.

"They look smashing, don't they?" Petra smiled, her anger and despair finally appearing to have subsided. "Really like they *belong*."

Elsa nodded. She just needed them to get around safely to confirm that it had been the right decision to step Merlin up a level.

It felt like forever until they came back into view, and Elsa gasped as they flew over the massive picnic table. She took a pull in time for the double of narrow brush fences, and tiring Merlin obliged with a shorter stride, and popped over them easily.

Sophia and Merlin stormed through the finish with just six time penalties. On a normal day, he would have easily made the time, but Sophia would have been going for a steady clear. Sophia clapped the gelding's neck, her smile as wide as Elsa's.

Elsa grabbed his reins, he was blowing but his ears were pricked, and he was searching her for treats.

"He was flying!" Elsa exclaimed.

"He felt amazing!" Sophia jumped to the floor and flew her good arm around the gelding's neck. "Like he'd been doing this level his whole life! I'm so glad we made the step up."

Elsa couldn't stop patting him and feeding him mints.

"He goes even better when I can only use one arm," Sophia laughed. "I think he likes being left alone."

"That reporter wants an interview," Elsa grinned, shoving Sophia towards a friendly-looking woman, Dictaphone and notebook poised as Sophia slid from the saddle.

Elsa unfastened Merlin's girth, and he was still nuzzling her, certain he had earned more carrots. Petra took his tack while Elsa walked him around, tipped a bucket of water over him and scraped off the excess to help him cool down. She threw a blanket over his quarters and walked him a couple of circuits around the lorry park until his breathing was back to normal, and they ambled slowly back to the barn.

"I'm so relieved that's over!" Sophia grimaced, stripping off Merlin's drenched and mud-coated protective boots, while Petra was out of earshot.

Elsa nodded in understanding. While there would be no placing for them, at least Merlin's record would show that he had completed his first ever Novice and he hadn't done too shabby.

Elsa gave him a well-earned hose down, dried him off and rugged him up. Drop Kick whinnied in delight at the return of his stablemate, and kicked the door in frustration. Elsa gave him a new haynet, hoping that would keep him occupied until it was time to head home.

"I think I'm going to get back," Sophia told her, clutching her elbow. "I'll never hear the end of it if I don't. Will you be alright getting finished on your own?"

"Of course," Elsa smiled. "You get some more painkillers inside you and get to bed. It won't get better without rest."

"Geez, you sound like my mother," Sophia rolled her eyes. "Are you sure..."

"*Go*," Elsa insisted, cutting her off.

"Thank you," she smiled. "Don't worry about the yard horses, Mum will do them. No need to hurry back."

"Great," Elsa smiled. "I think I might stay and watch the end of the two-star."

"Don't blame you, from what I hear Frederick has pretty much got it in the bag." Sophia retorted. "No doubt his face will be all over the big screen...*in close up*..."

Frederick. Elsa sighed. She hadn't seen him all day, and she would so *love* to see him again. She wondered if he wanted to see her again, or whether he'd decide she wasn't worth the fight she was putting up.

"I do hope you're not staying just to ogle the enemy, Elsa?"

Sophia grinned, observing her silence.

"Of course not!" Elsa blushed.

Once the horses were comfortable she retrieved Cecil from the lorry, and let him have a run in the woodland. She took Drop Kick out for a walk, and let him have a pick of grass before they started the journey home. The big grey gelding was still stiff, but grateful for a leg stretch, although Elsa was certain he had been mugging everyone that passed his stall for treats, and getting the sympathy vote.

She waited until she started seeing the top ten horses heading towards the warm-up, and called Cecil. She put Drop Kick away, checked their water and hay, and began the amble to the ring, Cecil annoyed that his Mum insisted on keeping him on the lead.

Elsa had chewed her nails down by the time it got to the final three. Being in the lead after the cross country, Frederick was the last to go on his huge, impressive black mare, Cavalier. She was torn between wanting him to knock every pole down and utterly disgrace himself, to flying round clear and in style and wiping seconds off the time.

The crowd gasped as Brett, laying in second, had a pole, making any chance of him landing the title seem impossible now. Elsa saw the heartache flash across Paige's face, and knew exactly how she felt. He gave his horse a pat as he finished within the time. And then the crowd were roaring as Frederick cantered in. He sat so softly, he looked so stylish and professional, that Elsa felt her heart lurch – like it must do for ninety percent of the females sitting alongside her. The remaining ten percent had something wrong with them, as far as she was concerned. Cavalier looked like she meant business. The pressure was on, and Frederick tipped his hat at the judge, and they were off.

Ava stood by the gate, hopping from foot to foot, riding every fence with her horse. She caught Elsa's eye, and waved.

Frederick barely seemed to move in the saddle. Cavalier sprung like a ping-pong ball, giving each fence inches and not looking one bit like she was suffering from storming around the earlier cross country course. There were gasps as Frederick turned tightly into the double, but he made it and kicked on.

There were only two fences left. Frederick was well up on the time; he just needed a clear and the title was his. He absolutely flew it, and the crowd were out of their seats, cheering, and Frederick punched the air with glee.

Even Elsa could see how much the win meant to him. Ava was jumping up and down, clasping her hands together.

"Well done!" Elsa hugged her. "You must be over the moon!"

"Absolutely! Bloody brilliant, isn't it?" Ava beamed, ecstatic.

She grasped hold of Cavalier's reins, she couldn't stop patting her, and the mare searched her for sugar lumps.

"You can have sugar, mints, extra carrots," Ava promised her, kissing her velvet nose. "You can have whatever you want!"

Frederick had dismounted and was surrounded by people wanting to talk to him. But even over the top of them he was looking right at Elsa. She felt her cheeks reddening under his gaze.

"Elsa," he said gently. Getting even a glimpse of her was better than any trophy he was about to receive.

"Well done," she smiled. *You deserve it*, she wanted to add, but she thought his ego already too big. She began to back away, grateful for the people that were surrounding him that stopped him from reaching out to her. He looked so different than when he had knocked on her lorry door. He'd had a sense of shyness and vulnerability about him then, a fun, teasing personality and likeability. But she didn't see it now that he was surrounded by these people – *his* people – who wouldn't give someone like her a second glance. He oozed arrogance and class; he had morphed back to the Frederick that she admired greatly at a distance for his unarguable skill and talent, the one who trampled over whoever he liked to get to where he was right now – and that was the Frederick she had no desire to get to know.

"I've got to go," she tugged on Cecil's lead. "Horses to box up, and all that. You know the score. Well done, again."

Merlin and Drop Kick walked enthusiastically into the lorry, happy to be heading home, and Elsa was quickly on her way. Once on the open road, she instructed her phone to call her mother, and turned the loud speaker up above the noise of the lorry cab. Long, lonely journeys were the best time for her to catch up with her loved ones.

"How's my best girl?" her mother answered excitedly. "I was beginning to wonder whether you were still alive!"

"Of course, I'm still here, Mum!" Elsa laughed. "I've been…"

"Yea, yea, busy," her Mum cut her off, and Elsa could sense her rolling her eyes.

"I wasn't going to say that!" Elsa replied. "I have been busy, *mega* busy, you're right. We've been competing at Napier this week, and it's been, well, *eventful*…excuse the pun."

"Oh," her Mum's attention was obtained. "I hope you have lots to tell me?"

"I do," Elsa smiled. She imagined her mother settling herself on the sofa of their cosy living room, her legs tucked under her as she snuggled up with a mug of coffee. Elsa recognised her subtle pang of homesickness; it was never far away every time she called her mother. "And I have a long journey home, so you'll hear the whole lot." She paused, and glanced across at the shiny trophy that Cecil was guarding on the passenger seat. She could not help the smile that lit up her face. "But firstly, I have the most *amazing* thing to tell you, Mum. You are not even going to believe what I won today…"

Chapter Six

Sophia was determined to be back in the saddle as quickly as possible. Only Petra stood in her way, and she was definitely a force to be reckoned with. Elsa had been keeping the horses ticking over all week, with just some gentle schooling and lots of hacking, and she'd barely had any spare time to think about Frederick and their night of...well, *nothing* together.

Aside from her handful of event horses, Sophia had two schooling liveries in too, for which Elsa also had to take up the reins temporarily. She liked a variety of riding, but the rest of the yard was suffering as a result of her increased workload. She had not swept the cobbles for days, the horses tack was filthy, and by the time she made it back to her cottage late into the evening, she was well and truly exhausted.

She had barely had the time or enthusiasm to ride Bear either, and the few times she had attempted it had been anything but a calm ride. Bear had tried to chuck her on several occasions; the worst time being in front of a dairy lorry, of which the driver was luckily very understanding. Elsa was beginning to contemplate whether getting a youngster had been a good idea, especially at the start of the season. Now they were mid-way through and she had not even accomplished half of what she'd planned with the tricky little mare.

"Picton is on next weekend," Sophia said casually, as the pair mixed up feeds.

Elsa stopped stirring, and looked up expectantly. "Yes?"

Sophia shrugged. At least she could do that now without it hurting. "Well, Merlin, Connor and Ruby are already entered. It would be a shame to withdraw them when they're all going so well."

"And what does Petra say?"

"As if I've discussed it with her," Sophia rolled her eyes. "I'm not that brave, Elsa."

Elsa was sweeping back the bed to her last stable when Colin drove past in the tractor, and she gave Sophia's father a friendly wave. She was so tired she couldn't wait to get inside and sit down. She knew as soon as her legs hit the sofa she wouldn't be able to get up again. It had been a long week keeping all the horses ticking over single-handedly, but Sophia had had a gentle ride this morning and said she felt up to it again. Tomorrow Sophia would take over some of the schooling again, and Elsa had no doubts that she'd be ready to compete at Picton.

Elsa just needed to fill a couple of haynets and then she could get Drop Kick in. He was still off work as he was a bit stiff, she'd tried to put him on the horse-walker but he'd proceeded to kick it to pieces, so she'd turned him out with the cows instead. He'd been standing by the gate for the last twenty minutes, with his woe-is-me face on. Elsa couldn't win; the minute she got him in he'd be banging on the door wanting to be let out.

"Elsa!" came a frantic shout from across the yard. "*Elsa!*"

Elsa dropped her broom and started running in the direction of the noise. Colin had stopped the tractor, and was leaning over the five-bar gate. Drop Kick was well and truly tangled in the stock fence, and panicking, despite Colin's best efforts to calm him.

"Steady, boy," Elsa said calmly as she approached him. "*Whoa.*"

He whinnied and tried to reach her, but he couldn't move. His eyes rolled in terror and he tried to rear. *Thank God I left his head collar on,* she thought, as she instinctively grabbed it, and he immediately calmed as she scratched his chin.

"I only turned him out for half an hour," she told Colin. "He was doing my head in kicking the door."

"Horses, eh?" Colin gave a gentle laugh. "I told Sophia not to bother with them. But would she listen?"

Elsa wanted to cry. She had *so* been looking forward to getting into her cosy cottage and snuggling up with Cecil. Now that looked like it was a long way away. Drop Kick had pulled his turnout boots off, and the one front shoe that was still attached to his hoof, had a strand of wire between the metal and his hoof. He had barbed wire wrapped around his knee, and he was dripping with blood. The more he panicked, the more it tightened.

Elsa ran her hand through her hair. "We're going to need some wire cutters and a vet," she sighed.

"Right you are," Colin gave her a nod. He returned with Sophia, Petra and two pairs of wire cutters. While Sophia held the geldings head and tried to keep him quiet, Elsa and Petra tried to hold his legs up in turn and free as much of the wire so that Colin could cut the reminder away.

Drop Kick limped sheepishly onto the yard, and Sophia held him while Elsa washed him down, watching the endless red water wash down the drain until the vet's pickup pulled into the yard.

"Evening," Harry greeted them, not looking at all amused. "He's certainly been in the wars recently this one, hasn't he?" His gaze lingered longingly on Sophia, and even Elsa managed a smile as Sophia's gaze dropped to the floor. She wished the pair of them would just admit their obvious feelings for each other and get on with it. Harry had been smitten with Sophia since his first ever visit to her yard, but they both appeared to lose the ability to speak properly when around each other.

"He sure has," Elsa replied eventually with a nod, and Harry knelt down to examine him. Elsa and Sophia waited with baited breath.

"Most are just superficial," he said eventually. "But that

one," he paused and pointed, and both Elsa and Sophia winced, "is almost down to the bone. I can't risk stitching any infection in. It's going to need dressing, and he'll have to have strict box rest and a course or two of antibiotics."

"Guess that's most of his season over then?" Sophia tried to hold back a threatening tear.

"It doesn't look good, I'm afraid," Harry straightened up, looking sympathetic. He wanted to throw his arms around her and comfort her, but she barely even looked at him.

He gave him a couple of injections, flushed the wounds out several times, and carefully bandaged them up. He was quiet while he worked, and for that Elsa was grateful.

"He'll need walking to stop the fluid building up," Harry instructed once finished. "Keep the dressing clean, and absolutely no turn out. You can't risk it getting infected." He handed Sophia a pile of antibiotics, making sure his hand touched hers as he passed them over. "These should keep you going for a while. I'll call in to check on him again next time I'm passing, maybe in a couple of days."

"Thanks, Harry," Sophia murmured gratefully, and Elsa noticed the crimson tint to her cheeks with a smile.

It was almost dark when she crawled back into her cottage, which for a summers night, was almost unheard of – not unless she had fallen asleep on the sofa before doing her evening check on the horses. Cecil ran straight to his bowl and looked up at her with longing, hungry eyes. She emptied out half a tin of meat for him, and headed straight for the shower. She slipped straight into her fleece dressing down, and only came back downstairs because Cecil was barking persistently at the door.

Petra stood on the doorstep, holding a cling film wrapped plate.

"Sorry it's not very exciting; dinner got put on hold with the drama," she told her sadly. "But I have rustled you up a chicken salad. You must be starving."

"Thank you *so* much," Elsa sighed. "Right now, I could happily chew on cardboard I am that famished."

"I didn't think you'd have any energy left to start making anything," she let herself in. "I bet you were going to go straight to bed on an empty stomach, weren't you?" she asked accusingly.

Elsa slowly nodded; she was no good at lying. "But now if I'm going to eat, I can treat myself to wine, can't I?" she held up a bottle of red. "Care to join me for a glass?"

"Oh, go on then," Petra smiled. "I think you've definitely earned a glass!"

"I think a *glass* is quite refined for me – I normally just skip the glass and have the bottle!" Elsa laughed, Petra watching as she poured two generous servings and they clinked glasses. Petra looked around as she stood in the kitchen; she'd always admired how homely Elsa had made her little cottage.

"Don't you ever get lonely here?" she asked thoughtful.

"No, I have all the company I need," Elsa replied without hesitation, her trusty companion by her side.

"I suppose it's OK while you're young, but you won't want this forever. We worried about you when you first took the job on; you were very young. You still *are*."

"Sophia was my friend," Elsa shrugged. "I knew I'd be very happy working for her, and you and Colin."

"And we love having you, but isn't it so time consuming? You never have a chance to get out and let your hair down, what about finding yourself a nice young man?"

She gave a gentle laugh. "I don't have time for silly stuff like that."

"Exactly," Petra looked concerned. "You work too hard. You need to stop working on your days off and get out there. You don't want to be old and lonely, trust me. There must be plenty of nice boys around here."

"I wouldn't know," Elsa smiled, "I've not had a boyfriend

since Luke Andrews!"

"Oh, good God!" Petra looked appalled. "Luke from school?"

Elsa nodded.

"Well, he was never marriage material, was he?"

"No, but there's plenty of time for all that, isn't there?" Elsa laughed.

"As long as you're happy, that's all." Petra sighed. "We do worry about you."

"I'm fine, honestly." Elsa insisted. She was twenty-six, and the thought never even crossed her mind. "There is no need to worry."

"Talking of worry... this is not going to be much of a season for you, is it? Now that our next top horse is off. Suppose we can't blame bloody FT for this one, can we?"

"Suppose we can't," Elsa agreed reluctantly.

"Christine Forrester was really winding me up at Napier, when I had the misfortune of bumping into her. Bragging to me and whatever friend of the moment was clinging to her, that FT had seen Nobby perform and absolutely demanded to have him in his stable yard. And who would ever turn down FT? Makes you sick, doesn't it? Still, we must not be bitter."

Elsa took a sip of her wine.

"What's up with you?" Petra demanded suspiciously, having expected her to fly off the handle. "Your rage towards FT seems to have subsided a little. Are you OK?"

"Of course," Elsa replied, blushing. "I'm just all-raged out, that's all." She took another sip of wine, and luckily Petra didn't seem to notice her awkwardness.

"I'm not sure if she's really up to competing this weekend." Petra changed the subject.

"Wild horses wouldn't keep her away." Elsa smiled, her discomfort subsiding a little as the conversation returned to familiar ground.

Elsa wasn't so keen on the selling horses part of her job. It wasn't so much the parting with them; she loved to see them going off to a lovely, new home and she couldn't deny the relief of having one less to muck out. But she hated the whole rigmarole of getting horses ready for people who had no intention of actually turning up to try them, or those that absolutely fell in love with the horse, couldn't find fault with it, yet offered them an offensive figure well below the asking price, and its market value. Ultimately, the money side was down to Sophia, but Elsa still found it to be a kick in the teeth to all the hard work she'd put in.

She took a sip of her fruit juice, glad that she had added the ice cubes, and relaxed in the gentle breeze that blew across her tiny patio. Her garden was barely that; actually a tiny paved area with enough room for a single table and chair, with a low brick wall topped with trellis to separate her from the grazing cows. But above the trellis were beautiful, uninterrupted views of the valley, which made this her most favourite place to sit.

Her mobile phone chirped, and she checked the display; a potential buyer who was coming to try Monty for the second time, just confirming that she would be arriving in twenty minutes.

Elsa had a good feeling about this one. Monty had originally been bought for Sophia to compete, but it had quickly become apparent that – despite having heaps of ability – he hadn't the enthusiasm for eventing, and would therefore be better suited to a private home with a little less pressure; either a one-to-one or a mother and daughter share, where he could bundle through a variety of riding club activities at his own pace. He excelled at all three eventing disciplines individually, but they had quickly found out at his first event, that he detested having to do them all on the same day.

Elsa quickly downed her drink, winced with the sudden brain freeze she was met with, and got to her feet.

Monty behaved perfectly for his rider, as he always did. He was as genuine as they came, and as safe as houses. He did everything that his rider asked – never any arguments – but there was no sense of urgency with him. He carried out every transition as if he had all the time in the world. There was no sharpness about him, and it had always frustrated Sophia a little. He would never make the time across country, and he'd never win a jump-off; Monty thought tight-turns to jumps were wholly unnecessary when he could simply go the long way and get a good run up.

He would, however, stay all day out hunting with your fragile Granny on board, and clear the biggest of walls and hedges, and Elsa knew you couldn't put a price on that. She loved hacking him out on a loose rein and letting her concentration lapse, knowing he'd always bring her home in one piece. It was refreshing after being aboard some of the sharper horses in Sophia's yard.

Martine was beaming from ear to ear as she pulled Monty to a halt, and didn't look like she ever wanted to dismount.

"I love him, Mum!" The teenager threw her arms around his neck, as she looked across to the rails for confirmation.

"Well, if you're sure," her mother shrugged, but could not hide her smile. "He seems ideal."

"He is! He *really* is," Martine gushed, and Elsa left Sophia to talk about money.

She saddled up Connor, put a bridle on Bear and headed out along the lanes, Bear trotting obediently alongside them. All of their horses were used to ponying or being ponied, and Elsa often led two to save time, but she didn't risk that when one of them was Bear.

When she finally returned to the yard, Martine and her mother had departed. Monty was to be delivered to his new home in two days' time, and although Elsa would miss him, she was equally excited for him. He would relish being the centre of a teenager's attention, and his sale brought in vital income to ensure that Sophia and her horses made it to their next event.

By the time it came to boxing the horses up for Picton, Sophia was more than ready to compete again. Merlin's high-exuberance had really put her shoulder through its paces the day before, and she decided if she could still move when she woke up the next morning, then she could tackle the big, strong cross country course that Picton was famed for.

Elsa's three horses travelled comfortably, and she settled them all in their stables in the main barn. After emptying her tack boxes from the lorry, she took Cecil for a walk to check out the arena.

"Have you come to snatch the best turned out yet again, Miss Aldridge?" Ava purred.

"Hey, stranger!" Elsa swung around to meet her, and they embraced in a friendly hug. "And of course not, it was a pure fluke at Napier!"

"There was no fluke about that," Ava told her from under raised eyebrows. They ordered a coffee from the catering van, and took a seat looking out over the trade stands setting up. "Your horses looked absolutely amazing, as they always do. Even Frederick noticed."

"Frederick?" Her head shot up.

"Yes, *Frederick*," Ava grinned. "I knew that would get your attention. So, you're not immune to him, after all?"

"I'm not sure I like the sound of Frederick noticing my horses," Elsa noted fearfully.

"Don't fret, we've got enough. But as it happens, we're looking for a new groom. We're always short staffed; he has very high expectations. We could do with someone just like you."

"Oh!" Elsa was surprised. "That's very sweet, but I'm more than happy at Sophia's."

"I thought you'd say that, but if you ever change your

mind..." she pressed. "It's a fantastic opportunity, chance for international travel and to work with and ride some of the best horses on the eventing circuit."

"Thanks," she smiled, gratefully. "But at the moment I hope I will have those opportunities at Sophia's."

"And I'm sure you will," Ava smiled, not doubting it for a moment, "but you can't blame a girl for trying, can you? And I can't think of anyone better that I'd rather work with." She stood up. "I'm just going to nip to the saddler's trade stand, I ordered a new headcollar that I need to pick up. I'll be back in five if you're heading back to the barn?"

"Sure," Elsa smiled, and watched her leave. Cecil sat on her feet, in no hurry to move. She would enjoy this five minutes of peace before she had to get back and start preparing her horses. This weekend would be non-stop.

Cecil barked, and Elsa looked up with a start at the man that had wandered in front of her. The exceedingly good-looking, tall man, who looked right at her with beautiful, soft blue eyes and made her heart skip vital beats.

Oh God, there he was. He was looking right at her, and she could have melted under his gaze.

"Elsa," Frederick purred, his blue eyes twinkling. "What a lovely surprise."

"Yes," she struggled to find her voice.

"I came to get a tea," he explained, even though she hadn't asked. "Actually, my groom was supposed to be getting me one, but she seems to have got distracted."

"She's gone to pick up a new headcollar," Elsa nodded towards the trade stands.

"Ah, yes, for that horse of hers. Honestly, she looks after that better than she looks after herself."

"I think the same could be said for most grooms," Elsa smiled.

He pulled out the seat beside her and sat down. Elsa looked at him in surprise, waiting.

"Sorry, can I join you?" he looked at her from under raised eyebrows. "Where are my manners?"

She could have sworn he sounded slightly nervous, as if she might say no. He really was a mystery to her.

"Well you've already sat down now," she smiled sweetly, unable to resist his boyish grin.

He nodded, and his smile returned. "A new week, time to try again."

"Try what again?" she frowned, her stomach already fluttering.

"Can I take you to dinner?" he asked quickly, before he had a chance to bottle it.

"Sorry what?" she gawped at him.

"I said," he spoke more slowly this time, amusement tugging at the corners of those gorgeous, kissable lips. "Can I take you to dinner?"

"You don't give up, do you?" Elsa laughed, barely trusting herself to speak. "Maybe your own groom would like to be taken to dinner?"

"But I don't want to take her," Frederick reasoned. "Besides I'm sure she can get something in the canteen."

"Is that how you treat your staff?" Elsa folded her arms across her chest, eyebrows raised at him accusingly. "And there she was, sitting just there trying to persuade me to come and work for you!"

"She was?" he looked surprised. He wasn't sure he'd ever get any work done himself if she was gracing his stableyard.

"Yes, but don't worry, I'm happy where I am." Elsa gave him her sweetest smile.

"Well, that's a relief then, isn't it?" He smiled, amused. "So, dinner?"

"No, Frederick." She struggled to decline, but she knew she must. She forced herself to look away, ran a hand through her loose hair, hating herself.

She didn't think she could ever forget the heartache she'd

felt, the day after they'd been on such a high for Nobby and Sophia's top ten finish in a three-star competition. Sophia had tearfully told her that Christine Forrester had just been on the phone, to inform her that Frederick Twemlow had been begging for the ride on Nobby, and a rider of that calibre was not one you turned down.

Elsa had felt like she'd been punched in the stomach. Just when he was beginning to show the world what he had to offer, Nobby would never compete for their stable ever again. And it was all Frederick's fault. Never content with having everything a normal person could only ever dream of, he had taken away to most important horse in the world to her. Frederick Twemlow had already taken away a Nobby-sized chunk of her heart, and not even his exceptional good looks and easy charm would ever get her to forget that.

"Oh," his smile fell, and he studied her. "Why do I get the impression you are still not exactly happy with me?"

"Who do you think you are?" She demanded, her raised voice taking even herself by surprise. "You think you can click your fingers and everyone jumps?"

"No, not at all." He looked quite offended. She was feistier than he thought, but it only made him more determined.

"Suppose you're used to getting your own way?" She went on accusingly, her happy memories of Nobby fuelling her venom. She refused to fall for his easy charm, refused to fall into his bed.

"Didn't get my own way the last time we met, did I?" he frowned. "I was very respectful of you, didn't touch you once, did I?"

"What do you want from me, Frederick?" she sighed. Cecil was on his feet, his hackles raised. "First the text, what was that all about? Don't you think us grooms work hard enough without traipsing around after horses that aren't in our care anymore? *Especially* when there is nothing wrong with them."

"OK, that was foolish of me," he looked around casually,

hoping no one was watching. The last thing he wanted was to draw attention to himself. "But let me make it up to you? I'd just like to take you out for dinner. Tomorrow night." He wanted to get her away from the event, where they could both relax and he could get to know her.

"Frederick, I'm a *groom*. I'm going to be hectic tomorrow night."

"It's OK; you'll have an extra pair of hands. I'll get Ava to help you."

"What? *No!*" her head was in turmoil. Her loyalty was to her employer and her horses, but dinner with Frederick Twemlow? She hoped she could forgive herself when he got bored of asking, because there was *no* way she was giving in.

"Actually, I'm not taking no for an answer," he said gently, his eyes confidently holding hers. "I'll pick you up at eight by the gates at the back of the stabling. We'll go somewhere close. We'll be a couple of hours' maximum; your horses won't even notice you've gone. And if they need anything, Ava will do it." He paused, but cut her off before she could object. "And before you ask, no I won't click my fingers at her, I'll ask her nicely. Ava won't say no. She's obviously better trained than you."

"I thought my ears were burning," came the Australian from behind them, and Elsa prayed that she had not heard much of their conversation. But the danger of the situation had her heart racing in disloyal and unwanted excitement.

"Unlike my tea," Frederick smiled, standing. "Which would be stone cold by now had you even bought it."

"Ah, yea, shit. Sorry, boss." She shrugged, not trying very hard to look sorry.

"I take that bit back," he turned to Elsa. "She's obviously not trained at all."

"I'll get you one now, boss," Ava smiled sarcastically.

"Don't bother," he told her breezily, a gentle prod in her chest. "*You'll* have to queue."

Both girls watched as he went to join the end of the small queue, and was quickly ushered to the front by some star-struck ladies, was handed a piping hot tea, and was sauntering away with a quick wink in their direction while females drawled after him, before Ava had even had a chance to sit back down.

"He is *so* arrogant," Elsa gazed after him. "Is he going to be pissed at you all day now?"

"He's really not," Ava laughed. "And of course he won't. He's teasing. I told you, you've got it all wrong about him."

"I'm intrigued," Elsa felt her heart beat slowing now that he had gone. "Tell me about the real him." *Please, tell me about this person I have just been coerced into going to dinner with*, her mind screamed at her.

"OK well, he's definitely not as arrogant as everyone seems to think." She took a deep breath as she retook her seat on the plastic chair for a moment before their non-stop day properly began. "People seem to have this misconception of him being big-headed, loud, rude and throwing his weight around. He's not, and he doesn't. He's privileged, but so what? There's a lot to be said for coming from wealthy, influential, successful parents – and it's sad, but he's never lived up to their high expectations. We both know that in this game you can have the best horse in the world, doesn't mean any old fool can ride it. He works really hard; he's *very* focused and doesn't like distractions. He's a perfectionist, and he expects the same from his staff. He doesn't seem to have lots of friends, and it's not because he's cocky and full of it – but actually he's private and shy."

Elsa's eyebrows rose. "Sorry, I was trying to believe the whole thing, but *shy*?"

"I know, and he'd hate me for telling anyone, but it's true. He tries so hard to hide it. But he's never alone because he's an arsehole to hang out with, Elsa. I spend a lot of time with him, I should know. He's dubious of people only wanting to hang out with him because he's got money, he's been like it ever since school apparently."

She nodded, absorbing this food for thought. But there was always another thought that sprang to mind every time she looked at him. "So, do you ever just look at him and wonder what he'd be like in bed?" Elsa teased.

"Hell yea! Every day, Elsa." Ava laughed. "But I also know how much I'd miss my horses if I took my eye off the ball, because he'd get shot of me in a flash."

"Is he single?" she probed casually.

"I've no idea." She shrugged. "He's never brought any female admirers into the yard as far as I know, but you never know what goes on behind closed doors. Especially in that big house of his."

Big house was an understatement; the Twemlow mansion was more of a stately home, and rumour had it that Frederick had his own wing.

"He's not short of admirers, is he?" Elsa bit her lip, noticing how the ladies in the queue still gawped after him, faces flushed.

"No, and I've a feeling I'm sitting next to one right here," Ava gave her a wink.

"Oh, *please*," Elsa rolled her eyes, carefully averting her gaze. As soon as Frederick was out of sight, Cecil relaxed. His hackles went back down and he curled up on her feet. "Plus, my dog can't seem to stand him, and that's the only indication I need, isn't it?"

She'd make it perfectly clear to him over dinner, just how disinterested in him she really was, she told herself defiantly, even though her heart screamed at her that that would be an idiotic thing to do.

Eventually they stood, and began the walk back to the barn in the early sunshine. It was already warm, and Elsa was glad she had been brave and put her shorts on, even if the whiteness of her legs did scare the horses.

She couldn't believe she had agreed – in a roundabout way – to go out for dinner with Frederick Twemlow. She couldn't believe his persistence for someone as plain as *her*, when he could surely have anyone. She so wanted to tell Ava, but she knew it was probably better for their friendship if she didn't. Elsa didn't want her thinking she was just like all the other girls, desperate to get closer to Frederick and using her as a stepping platform. Ava had become a firm friend, and Elsa didn't want to lose that. She also hated not telling her. But if Frederick was going to ask her to keep a check on her horses, surely she'd put two and two together.

"Ava, I know this show is manic for both of us, but please can I ask you a favour?"

"Of course, girl." Ava replied without hesitation. "I owe you, so what's the problem?"

"I have to go out tonight. At eight. Please could you keep an eye on my horses?"

"Sure." She narrowed her eyes at her suspiciously. "What kind of out?"

"Like a dinner...*out*," Elsa replied cautiously.

"Oh, my *God!*" Ava squealed excitedly. "You got a hot date? Tell me who with!"

"It's not a hot date!" Elsa laughed, feeling her cheeks warming. "It's just an old friend who lives around here. He asked me unexpectedly."

"But it is a *he*..." Ava probed. "But unexpectedly? Does that mean you don't have anything to wear?"

"I don't, you know?" Elsa gasped, realisation suddenly hitting her. "Oh, *shit!*"

"It's OK, come to my lorry beforehand to get ready. You're the same size as me, I'll dig you something out."

"You bring nice clothes away to shows with you?" Elsa frowned, admiring her.

"Well, yea." Ava shrugged, with a roll of her eyes. "When

you're Fred's groom and he wins all these fancy awards and gets invited to all these fancy events, and he has no one to take and his mum is otherwise unavailable, it pays to have a couple of decent dresses and a makeup bag on the lorry, know what I'm saying?"

Elsa smiled. *Of course*, she had no idea how the other half lived.

Elsa did make sure that at least her horses looked fit to hang around with the equine celebrities of Picton, however, and Connor's sleek dappled grey coat shone as he and Sophia entered the arena for the dressage. He was the one Sophia had been most worried about, and so Elsa was glad he was going first. He had not performed in front of a decent crowd before, and the gelding's eyes were on stalks as Sophia encouraged him forward. Elsa was pleased he was so genuine and honest and tried his hardest to look after his rider, and despite the number of mistakes they accumulated that put them right at the lower end of the leader board, it had been a good first experience for Connor, and that was all that a groom and rider could really ask of a young horse.

Elsa jumped on him to cool him off, and walked him back to the stables. Such was the order of the day that there was little time between Connor's dressage and show jumping time, and Elsa would need to work in Ruby as Sophia had to be immediately back in the ring for her dressage test. Merlin was not running until tomorrow, so luckily that made the logistics a little easier.

She gave Connor another brush over and changed him into his jumping tack. Then she legged Sophia back into the saddle and set about getting Ruby brushed and plaited for her dressage.

Three poles down put Connor well out of contention, but Ruby was impeccable in her dressage, putting her straight into third place. Ruby was not so into the show jumping, and had two poles down which Sophia was furious at herself for.

"Looks like we'll be doing some grid work when we get back home," Derek smiled as she trotted out of the ring. "But don't fret; they've both got potential to be really nice jumpers. At the moment, they're both just getting a little close."

Sophia nodded. She knew she had a long way to go, but with her determination, she knew she would make it. She handed the reins gratefully to Elsa, and ran off to get changed.

Back at the barn, Elsa checked both horses over for correctly fitting tack, checked their studs and greased their legs. There would be no rosettes today, but a steady, flowing, fault-free run across country for both of them would be the same thing in her eyes. They had bright futures; there would be plenty of time for rosettes for them.

Chapter Seven

"Get in that shower, *now!*" Ava shoved her into the bathroom before she was barely through the lorry door. "I'm not saying you stink, but seriously, if you haven't seen this guy for a while, you want to be sure to show him what he's been missing!"

"He's just an old friend," Elsa insisted, but there was no point in trying to convince Ava, who's mind on the matter was firmly made up - or even to try and convince herself – and instead she tried to borrow some of Ava's excitement and enthusiasm.

"Do I have time to wash my hair?" Elsa frowned. "I *really* need to wash my hair."

"Yes!" Ava grinned. "Wash your hair; I will do something fantastic with it." She paused, handed her a bundle of towels and a wash bag. "Take these – there's shampoo and conditioner and shower gel. Oh, and a new razor – you probably don't want to use Fred's. Or you do, who knows." She gave a wink.

Elsa liked her. She wanted to hug her, but instead she stepped into the pristine shower and made the most of the luxury of the warm, powerful shower that was almost like being at home. When staying away at shows, Elsa was restricted to using the communal showers, and they were nothing as glorious as this.

"This lorry is absolutely divine," she said, when she eventually stepped out and looked around in awe. The kitchen was bigger than that in her own cottage, and the pop-out sides made the interior seem massive. The colour scheme was shades of blue, and everything matched, even the cushions piled on the sofa, that Elsa dread to think how much it must have cost.

"It's pretty swish, isn't it?" Ava grinned, stretching out across her excessively comfy chair. "You sure I can't tempt you with that job offer?"

"Let's see what you can do with my hair first!" Elsa laughed.

As it turned out, Ava's talents with hair stretched way beyond horses. Elsa sat across her bed while Ava tamed the caramel locks with the hair dryer and brush into huge curls that bounced on her shoulders.

She delved into her makeup bag. "I'll do it quite subtle," she murmured as she brushed powder over Elsa's gentle freckles. "I don't want to overdo it, you're so..."

"No, don't give me that *you're so naturally pretty anyway* bullshit," Elsa cut her off. "Slap it all on – the more I've got to hide behind the better."

"No way!" Ava laughed. "Let him see *you*." She added a touch of mascara, a tab of blusher to bring colour to her cheeks, and leant back to admire her good work.

"You'll do," she smiled, and passed her a mirror.

"I'll do?" Elsa laughed, eyebrows raised in surprise. "I don't think I've ever looked this good!"

"I'm a girl of many talents!" Ava laughed, making for the wardrobe. "Now for a dress."

Elsa was glad she'd been wearing her shorts as much as British summertime allowed, and hoped her legs wouldn't look too pasty compared to the rest of her. But she hadn't been planning on wearing a dress anytime soon.

Her size almost perfectly matched Ava, except that Ava was slightly shorter, so dresses came up a bit further above the knee on Elsa.

"I'm sure he won't mind that," Ava laughed, as Elsa tried to pull the hem lower.

"I do! I want to look classy – not desperate!" Elsa retorted, wondering if this was all a bit too much. She knew she should put in less effort if she really didn't want him to like her, but she couldn't bring herself too. All of her senses were imploring with her to look *amazing*.

"No one could mistake you for desperate," Ava told her.

Elsa didn't like the red dress that Elsa was trying to persuade her to keep on. It was frilly and showed too much cleavage for her liking, and it was *bright, really bright*.

"Fine," Ava eventually sighed in defeat, as Elsa tugged it off over her head. "The failsafe LBD it is, then."

Elsa *loved* it. It was sleek and clung to her in all the right places. It was low cut but the upper half was black lace detail over a lighter fabric. And it was short but still stylish with a subtle sequin design along the lower hem.

"Good *God!*" Frederick exclaimed, almost tumbling backwards off the lorry steps. "I'm sorry, but have we met before?"

Elsa felt her cheeks flaming, as she spun to greet him, looking aghast. Neither of the girls had even heard him open the lorry door.

"Elsa's got a hot date, boss." Ava grinned.

"Has she now?" he regarded her with approval. "Well, he's a very lucky guy indeed."

"Ava is kidding," she stammered, struggling to read his reaction. "It's not a *hot date*; it's just dinner...with a friend."

"Babe, it's a date and you know it!" Ava winked. "Now get out of here! Your horses will be fine – I'm going to the barn soon – I'll check on them. And good luck!"

"Yes," Frederick said quietly, his breath catching as he took in the beautiful sight before him. She looked as good as he had envisioned, out of her exceptionally seductively tight-fitting yet tatty yard jeans and grubby t-shirts. And he had envisioned her a lot recently, but he had never imagined in his wildest dreams that he could encourage her to go out to dinner with him. He had feared he was making her attend under duress, but surely someone who didn't *want* to go to dinner with him, didn't let themselves look so beautiful for the event? He licked his lips as he silently speculated that she must be interested in him after all – although she tried so hard to convince them both that she wasn't – because she was looking well and truly sizzling *hot. And all of this is for me*, he had to restrain himself from reaching out and touching her. He felt like a kid in a sweetshop. Stepping aside, he watched her exit. "Good luck." He murmured, and he couldn't wait to get around to those gates and pick her up.

Elsa walked slowly; wondering how long Frederick would need to get ready to go to dinner, when he always looked fabulous anyway. She didn't want to go back to her own lorry and face one hundred questions from Sophia. She was glad she'd brought her long, thin cardigan, for it was too warm for a coat, but a girl in a sexy black dress didn't entirely fit in here, and she drew some glances from people relaxing and drinking outside their lorries in the evening sunshine.

The worn path from the lorry park to the temporary stabling was always busy, and Elsa walked quickly, self-conscious and wishing she were back in her shorts and t-shirt, rucksack on her back and sweat sheets slung over her arm.

She waited around the corner of the barn, trying to look casual as she leaned back against the wall, and not give any signs that actually her stomach was churning and she was so nervous she needed to wee again even though she'd been just before she left. She pulled her phone from her bag and scrolled through her social media pages. Her old friends from her life before grooming for Sophia were posting pictures of their barbeques in the sun, or the getting ready and pre-drinks before hitting the town, and her heart gave a little pang. But she couldn't help but smile. Although she missed them, she wouldn't change her life now for anything in the world. Yes, she was often exhausted and she had to work outside in all weathers, and when a horse in her care was being particularly unruly she did sometimes wonder why she bothered, but now here she was at an event that Sophia had worked bloody hard to get to, her horses looked great, and now she was about to head for dinner with the most good-looking, eligible bachelor on the eventing circuit. Any girl would be envious; she just needed to calm her nerves. She needed to put Nobby and her loyalty to Sophia out of her mind for just one night. She deserved this impending evening of fun without feeling guilty. She had tried to say no, after all.

She looked up at the sound of an engine and his Range Rover pulled to a halt before her. His personalised plate informed her immediately that it was him, and the luxurious vehicle and its roaring engine screamed money and class. She gave a gentle smile, and he climbed out and came to open the door for her.

"It's OK," she giggled nervously, "I can open the door myself!"

"I know," he smiled, not letting her. "But I want to." He wore a crisp blue shirt, with a darker blue collar, square silver cufflinks, tight black jeans and killer leather shoes. She could stand looking at him all night. But he was waiting with the door open, a lopsided grin as his eyes roamed her.

She climbed in, trying not to let her dress ride up her leg too far, which was easier said than done.

"You look stunning, by the way," he told her, his eyes lingering on her. "I would have told you before – but – well, you know..." he trailed off, and she nodded, feeling her cheeks blushing already. He shut the door and climbed in beside her.

She felt so self-conscious sitting beside him, shuffling around in her dress. She noticed him stealing glances at her as they departed the lorry park. He looked so cool and collected, just like he did when he was about to head out on cross country. In fact, she thought he looked absolutely *divine*. And his curly hair sprang like he'd just ruffled it, and she longed to reach over and slide her fingers through it.

"I've booked us a table at a nice little Italian in town, I hope that's OK?" he enquired, with a bite of his lip, breaking her from her thoughts.

She nodded, studying him. Was he *nervous?* She found it hard to believe *Mr cool-and-collected* could ever be nervous.

"Sounds lovely," she smiled, her voice wavering.

A steward waved them out, and they hit the main road, through the pretty village and out onto the country roads that would take them to town. The engine roared as Frederick put his foot down, and Elsa was glad for the distraction from the silence.

"This is certainly plusher than my little Fiat," she commented, looking around at the vast and luxurious interior of the pristine Range Rover. Her little car was so cosy – debateable whether that was because it was just small or always full of junk – and Frederick suddenly felt so far away. She wasn't sure if she was grateful for this, or secretly disappointed, and she sank bank into the sleek, leather seat.

"Ah, yes, I've seen your little Fiat," he smiled, remembering the time he'd stupidly lured her to his yard.

"It's a banger, but it does the job," she said quietly. She struggled to get comfortable in her dress. She wanted to look relaxed and at ease, but she felt far from it. She was conscious of how fat her thighs looked when pressed against the leather seat, and she fidgeted. She straightened her posture and looked out of the window. Then suddenly feared she looked unsociable, and spun her head towards him.

He was watching her from the corner of his eye, an amused smile tugging at those luscious lips.

She silently cursed herself and chewed nervously on her fingernails, then remembered how her mother scolded her for it being such an unattractive trait, and delved her hands between her thighs to stop herself. This only made her dress ride up, and she frantically pulled it down.

"Please, relax," Frederick purred, his smile growing. "I'm really not that scary."

With a bite of her lip she folded her arms and resumed to the safety of looking out of the window, as the evening sunshine beat down on the recently harvested fields.

He must think I'm a blithering idiot, she told herself, feeling her cheeks burning. He didn't seem in a hurry to speak, and she hated the awkward silence. Why couldn't she be one of those funny, outgoing girls who always had something witty to say that had guys falling at their feet?

"It has sentimental value," she told him, not caring that she was babbling. "The Fiat. My grandpa gave it to me when he had to give up driving. It was my first car, and after he died I couldn't bear to trade it in. We've acquired a few scrapes over the years, but I think we've got the hang of it now."

"You must have, if Sophia lets you take charge of the lorry," he smiled, pleased that she was talking.

She turned to look at him, glad that their eye contact was quickly broken by him having to turn back to the road, and she could get a proper look at him.

"Well, it's easy driving that, isn't it?" she shrugged. "It's massive, and cars just get straight out of the way when they see a woman behind the wheel!"

He roared with laughter, and she quickly felt more at ease. *Maybe I can do funny,* she thought.

"Easy peasy," she added with a wink. "Nothing to it."

She felt his gaze bearing into her longer than he safely should. Her eyes followed his slender fingers as they reached towards her and found the gear stick, and she wished they'd keep going and find her thigh... He slowed the car as they approached the junction. His tongue swirled across his bottom lip as he watched for traffic, and then his foot was to the accelerator and the huge powerful car lurched forward. She smiled, settled back into her seat in comfort as he navigated the tight corners. *She could get used to this.*

"So, tell me about yourself."

She looked up in surprise. "Hmm? I'm really not that

interesting." She told him shyly.

"I wouldn't want your company if I thought that were true." He murmured, finding her intriguing.

"What is there to tell?" she turned back to the window. She was just a groom, not a high-achiever like him. Really, what was there to tell?

"OK, how did you come to be grooming for Sophia?" he asked, undeterred.

"We've been friends for years." She said quietly.

"So, how did you meet?"

"Why do you want to know?" she narrowed her eyes at him.

"Because I want to get to know you, Elsa," he laughed.

"OK, well..." she took a deep breath. She hated the silence, but she hated talking about herself even more. *Get a grip*, she told herself. "She was a couple of years below me at school, but I met her properly at the riding school. I was a pony-mad kid, spent every Saturday and Sunday of my childhood mucking out and tacking up to earn my half hour ride, and spending every spare minute with my favourite pony. Sophia had ponies at home, but used to come to the riding school for a weekly lesson. She asked me if I wanted to go to a show with her, I could tack up and help her warm up, and I never looked back from there really. I was never going to have a pony of that calibre of my own, so sharing Sophia's was the next best thing."

"That's a very sweet story," he smiled.

"Not as sweet as yours, no doubt," she held his gaze.

He didn't reply. He could only imagine what it would have felt like to have fun with ponies as a child; his parents had piled on the pressure to be the best of the best as soon as he'd taken an interest in something. His smile didn't even subside, and the longer the sudden silence stretched, the guiltier she felt. *He was being nice, what was her problem?*

He pulled into the town car park, and expertly manoeuvred into a parking space. She smoothed down her dress, determined not to lose any dignity while exiting the vehicle. Before she was ready, he was at her door and had opened it for her. She smiled, and stepped out. She expected him to move, but he stood right before her. Their bodies were almost touching, and she thought she might faint as she took a deep breath of how good he smelled.

His eyes searched hers. "We can be anything we want to be, Elsa" he murmured.

Her breath caught as she watched him, his eyes searching hers, and wandering down to her lips. But she couldn't read him, and then he backed away, and she felt cheated. She felt her heart beating hard in her chest, and needed to steady herself before she trusted her legs to walk.

They were quickly shown to their table, and she ordered the first thing her eyes saw on the menu – spaghetti Bolognese – thinking she couldn't really go wrong with that, but in reality, her stomach was turning somersaults and she didn't think she'd be able to eat even a mouthful. She wondered how he could manage to do that to her, with just one look?

"So, how is my best boy doing?" she asked him, anything to fill the awkward silence of him just, well, *looking* at her.

"I am doing very well, thank you for asking," he grinned back at her. "I had no idea you thought so highly of me already."

"Not you," she rolled her eyes. "Nobby! I notice he's not out this week. Picton is one of his favourite courses. I hope he is OK after last week?"

"Of course, he is fine," Frederick reassured her. "We have lots of competitions lined up for him, but this weekend he is chilling out in the field with his new friends."

"Oh!" Elsa immediately looked pleased, and Frederick wished he could make her smile like that more often; she really was so beautiful.

"Does he get much turnout, then?" she enquired, breaking

him from his thoughts.

"Of course, my yard is not a prison, Elsa," he told her, amused. "Horses only perform to the best of their capabilities when they are allowed to be...well, *horses*."

"I am so relieved!" clasping together her hands, she let out a breath she didn't realise she'd been holding. "Nobby loves his field, I was so worried about him being cooped up in a stall all day." She broke off, not wanting to speak out of turn. It was none of her business how he was kept anymore.

"You've no need to be worried," Frederick reassured her gently. "And you're always welcome to drop by and see for yourself."

"Can I?" her face lit up.

Ah, that smile again. "Of course," he'd agree to anything she wanted if it meant he got to see that smile. *Anything.*

Their food was served, and she twirled her spaghetti around her fork. She had been so hungry, but now, his handsomeness sitting opposite her, his brilliant blue eyes never leaving her, her appetite was gone. For food, anyway.

"Are you OK?" he asked gently, thinking how uncomfortable she suddenly looked.

She nodded a little too fast.

"You look amazing, by the way, did I tell you?" he swirled his tongue along his bottom lip.

She nodded. He had, four times, and she'd blushed every single time.

"That's Ava's dress." He commented a moment later, not struggling to tuck into his own meal.

She looked up. "How do you know?"

"She wore it to some awards dinner we went to once. Didn't look half as good as you do in it, though." He smiled.

She blushed again and turned her attention back to her plate. He always looked so natural; so *naturally perfect*. She couldn't look at him for too long without her stomach starting to flutter, and that wasn't at all helping with her sudden lack of appetite.

What did he want with her? What did he *see* in *her*? She didn't want to have dinner with him; she couldn't feel indebted to him. She *so* wanted to sleep with him, but she couldn't deal with the humiliation of him loving and leaving her. This was her livelihood, she was trying to forge a career here, she wanted to be respected and she certainly didn't want to be just another notch on Frederick Twemlow's assumedly-designer, expensive bed post.

"We can go," he said gently. "If you're uncomfortable, or not hungry?"

"No, I'm fine," she lied, twirling another strand of spaghetti half-heartedly around her fork.

She cursed herself. Why did she have to be so awkward? Why couldn't she just throw herself at him, go with the flow and be glad he showed her some attention, even if it was only until he got her into bed?

"Seriously," he stilled her twirling hand, his touch sending tingles down her spine. "Why don't we go somewhere else?"

"Like where?" she murmured, half hopeful yet half terrified.

"Anywhere of your choice? I wanted you to enjoy yourself, have a good time. You are clearly doing neither of those."

"Oh, God. I'm so sorry." She sighed, ran a frustrated hand through her perfectly styled, loose hair. "I must seem so ungrateful. It's not personal."

Then what is it? His beautiful blue eyes implored her. "Is the food not good?"

"It's lovely," she sighed. It really was; and in any other company she'd want to scoff two portions.

"But?" he smiled. "You're not a big eater?"

Oh! She was a massive eater, but not when he sat there, looking at her like that, making her stomach turn somersaults. She just wanted to launch across the table at him.

"You can tell me," he told her, that encouraging smile doing crazy things to her insides.

She shook her head. *And keep any sense of self-restraint and dignity?* Tell him that she couldn't eat a thing of this delicious meal because all she could think about was ripping his clothes off. Could she face the humiliation of giving her whole body to him, and him not so even as much as looking at her ever again?

She wondered, if she did let him get her into bed, would she remember what to do? It had been a while since she'd been intimate with anyone, even since anyone had seen her naked. She knew she'd let herself go a bit; her body wasn't her top priority these days, and while riding and yard work ensured she kept her size ten figure, she was partial to large servings of chips and cake after a tough day – or even after an easy day.

But doing her hair was reserved for very special occasions only, and yet she had done it tonight for him. Rather, she had let Ava do it, which was even more significant for her. Sometimes she went to the beauty salon, and got a manicure and pedicure, and a lot of waxing went on, and she felt fresh and vibrant and vowed to keep on top of their hard work, but it soon wore off. Nails chipped as soon as she came within close proximity of a horse. She'd always figured that if she ever found a guy she liked, they'd have to like her for who she was – beauty malfunctions included. She didn't think that would be acceptable to the immaculately preened Frederick.

So why had she attacked her legs and bikini line with the waxing strips before this weekend again, then, and slapped a bit of colour onto her chipped nails? Had she been hoping Fred would ask her out again? Of course she had – who was she kidding? Cecil couldn't care less if she lounged around looking like she'd been dragged through a hedge.

It was all for Frederick. He was the only one she'd been thinking about when she'd been dancing around the bathroom of her little cottage looking for waxing strips that hadn't dried out they were so out of date, while Cecil looked on – wondering what all the commotion was about and where the hell his dinner was. So why now, when he was sitting here before her, as gorgeous as ever, was she making such a mess of it?

"Tell me what's on your mind?" Frederick murmured.

She looked up sharply, felt her cheeks reddening.

"I can't," she whispered. "I'd die of embarrassment."

He smiled, and she broke into a gentle laugh.

"You are so adorable; you know that, don't you?" He brushed her cheek tenderly with his thumb, and she jumped at his touch.

She slowly shook her head, nervously bit her lip.

"And so difficult to read," he went on amused. "But I am determined. I will figure you out, Elsa. Give me time."

She dropped her fork. *Time?* "How much time, exactly? You don't want a one-night stand?" she regretted the words as soon as they left her mouth.

"What? Why would you think I do? Do you?" he was very amused. Of course, it had crossed his mind more than once that evening already how he could subtly remove Ava from his lorry so that he could take her back there, but the idea was a non-starter, unattainable for a dedicated groom and a focussed rider. And he had a feeling it would take a lot more than one simple dinner to get Elsa to want to go anywhere near him.

"No, of course I don't. But..." Elsa's cheeks were flaming. *Why the hell had she just said that?*

"I told you before, I would like to get to know you. Is it a crime wanting to get to know someone a little first?" he enquired. She intrigued him so much, and he sincerely wanted to get to know her. Anything that followed would be a glorious bonus. And he couldn't imagine being satisfied after just one night together; she would always leave him wanting more of her – much, *much* more of her.

Slowly she shook her head. Half of her wanted to kiss him

so bad, yet the other half wanted to run for the hills and never look back. She would never be in his league; she would always be just a little play thing for him, and she didn't think her young, inexperienced heart could cope with the heartache that would bring.

Yet, supposing Ava was right about him? That he wasn't any of the things she had been lead to – and allowed herself to – perceive him to be? What if he really was kind, quiet, sensitive...*shy*? What then? Oh, this was too much to think about.

"I should get back." She murmured, hastily dropping her fork again with a clatter. *What the hell is the matter with me?* She sighed.

"Stay at mine tonight?" he asked quickly, surprising even himself.

"I can't. We both know that I can't." She whispered, not feeling she had to list the reasons. There were too many of them; Ava, and the fact that he hadn't even kissed her yet. *Yet.* She couldn't face another sleepless night beside him, no touching.

He nodded. "Well, then, what are you doing next weekend?"

"I'm busy." She replied quickly.

Hurt flickered across his face. "Oh, I see." He signalled to the waiter for the bill. Elsa felt criminal; she had barely touched any of her meal, which for her was unheard of.

"No, sorry, I didn't mean that to sound so..." she trailed off. "I really am busy. I'm competing on Sunday; I want a clear head."

"*You* are?" His eyebrows were raised.

"*I* am, yes." She narrowed her eyes at him.

"Where?" he smiled, wondering why she hadn't mentioned it earlier. He felt that there was so much about her that she wouldn't mention.

"Nelson. I doubt I'll bump into you there, though." She

babbled. "In fact, I bet you've never even heard of it."

"I have heard of it, and I have competed there, too. We all have to start somewhere, Elsa." He said coolly.

"Even with tonnes of money and from a family of fancy titles?" she asked bitterly.

"Even with those," he replied quietly, hiding his amusement with his refusal to rise to the bait.

"God, I'm sorry." She groaned.

"Don't be." He paid, and stood, getting her cardigan for her and helping her into it. Almost every female in the room was looking at him, and Elsa felt so inferior. She longed to be back in her lorry, tucked up with Cecil. She didn't belong with Frederick, didn't belong anywhere with someone like him and sensed that most of the females in this restaurant thought it.

"We've been stuck in a bit of a rut recently. I've been so busy with Sophia," she prattled, anything to fill the awkward silence that had fallen between them. "We haven't really progressed much. Bear was fresh off the track six months ago. She was a bit of a handful, to say the least. She was heading for the meat man, so I took her."

"That's very admirable of you." He said quietly, holding the door for her on their way out.

She took a deep breath of fresh, summer evening air, and wished her nerves would calm. It was official; she had totally made a hash of things.

He opened the Range Rover door for her and watched as she climbed in. She gazed out of the window as they hit the road, trying to think of something...*anything* witty to say to ease the awkward silence. She didn't want to tell him about Bear; all of her big achievements with her would be so trivial to him. Hell, every part of her life was so trivial compared to his. She stole a glance across at him. He looked deep in thought.

"How about you?" she asked him, in her attempt to salvage anything of the evening. "Did you always want to be an eventer?"

He looked at her in surprise, although she noticed he tried his best to hide it. "*I* did, yes," he replied, a moment later, and she was sure she detected some sadness in his voice. "But no one else wanted me to be. My parents thought shovelling shit and cleaning tack was too lowly for *their* son."

Now it was her turn to look amused. "As if you ever shovelled shit and cleaned tack."

"We all have to start somewhere, Elsa." He murmured, not looking at her. "Do you think if my parents had gone out and bought me a stable yard of expensive horses, and handed everything to me on a plate, that I would be where I am now?"

She realised he was waiting for her answer, and she gave a gentle shrug. "I thought..." she trailed off, unsure of the words to choose.

"Everyone thinks that," he grunted, and now she definitely detected sadness. "Well, for the record, as soon as I showed any interest in ponies, they went out and bought me the most, expensive, flashiest horse they could find in Europe. And well, I couldn't ride it, could I? So, I gave up as quick as I'd begun, and they were mortified. They sold him and I went off to be a working pupil with a four-star eventer. I got the placement all by myself, and my parent's felt so shunned that they didn't provide me with anyone where horses were concerned, not until I started winning, and then I was the apple of my father's eye. But that's a whole different story." He broke off. He sounded bitter, and it scared her a little. "People overlook the work I put in to get here, Elsa, because I was an unknown then. But if you get handed everything on a plate, you don't have any determination to succeed, do you?"

She noticed his fist was clenched, and he tapped it irritably on the steering wheel. No one could fault his determination. And so, his eventing journey had not started with a stable yard of expensive, impressive, imported horses?

Wow, she turned to look out of the window, trying to

process it. His words conflicted with everything she'd ever thought about him, and she felt awful. She was suddenly desperate to know more about him, but he had gone cold on her, she noticed uncomfortably. She had had her chance, but she had well and truly stuffed up their evening.

"Can you drop me off at the barn? I want to cheek the horses." She murmured, noticing they were quickly nearing Picton.

Ever the gentleman, he parked up and came around to open her door. She smiled as he helped her out.

"Thank you," she told him, expecting him to go.

"That's alright. Can I help you with the horses or anything, you know, for ruining your evening with them?" His expression was unreadable; she failed to detect any amusement, any chance of a teasing smile.

"Frederick," she sighed. "My evening has been...great. Not ruined. I've had a nice time. Thank you – I mean it. And I'm sorry, for what I said."

She had definitely seen him in a different light. He was friendly, funny, even better good looking as the night fell if that was even possible, and she desperately wanted to see him again. But she knew, if anything, it had been *she* that had ruined it, and she inwardly cursed herself. She so wanted to be able to let her guard down and get to know him properly, but something stopped her. She knew, deep down, that she'd even love to spend all night with him, but of course they couldn't while she was pretty much living on top of Sophia in her lorry, and Frederick's – well, while spacious, it was not *that* spacious while Ava seemingly occupied much more than half of it.

He was staring at her, and she didn't know what to do. She was so inexperienced at these sorts of things – at *dating* – if that was what you could even call it. She turned on her heel, tipsily preceded towards the barn – the wine gone straight to her head on her empty stomach. She heard his heavy, hurried footsteps behind her. His hand had grasped her wrist and he shoved her back against the barn. She gasped as her bare back scraped the unforgiving brick wall. He had a palm either side of her head, there was nowhere for her to go. His mouth was just inches from her. Her heart was beating so fast. She took a deep breath of his aftershave, even with the manure-smell of their surroundings, he smelt divine.

"I don't like distractions, Elsa, so normally I don't have them. But you...what are you doing to me?" he breathed, his soft blue eyes searching her lips. He brushed a thumb across her lower lip, and she trembled. "I want to kiss you so bad."

"Kiss me, then," she whispered, waiting.

Slowly he shook his head. "No, I won't."

She tried to hide her surprise, her disappointment, but she failed miserably. "What?"

"I won't kiss you, because you think I'm an absolute prick. And I'm not, Elsa." He told her, his blue eyes clouding with a sadness she hadn't seen before. "I've tried not to be a prick to anyone in my whole life, so I'm not about to change the habit of a lifetime now. A prick is a prick, Elsa, it doesn't matter how long you make him wait. Three dates, three months – he'll still be a prick. *I'm not.*"

"Just kiss me, please?" she pleaded.

But he shook his head. "I admire that Ava has no idea who you were going out with tonight, I'm a private person and I'm happy that you seem to follow that trait. However, had you have told her, she would have quite rightly informed you that all these misconceptions you seem to have formed upon me, are exactly that – *misconceptions.*"

"She has already told me," Elsa hissed. "And I believe her. So please now just fucking kiss me!"

Chapter Eight

Frederick pulled away, frustrated, and ran his hands through that ruffled hair that she just wanted to delve into with her own palms and ruffle to oblivion while their tongues fought each other.

They both spun around to the sound of gentle footsteps. Elsa was surprised she heard them, so loud was her heart beating.

"Hey!" Sophia frowned, swinging around the corner of the barn. She slowed as she approached them.

"Hey," Elsa replied, flustered. "I've been out – I just came to check the horses."

"They're fine; I've just been in there. There are more grooms around than I thought they'd be. You guys don't stop, do you?"

"No rest for the wicked," Elsa gave a gentle laugh. She looked at Frederick loitering, but he wouldn't look at her. He looked so *hurt*. His lost expression tugged on her heart strings.

"I'm going to erm...head back," Sophia began awkwardly.

Elsa nodded. "Frederick..." she began, but he had already turned on his heels and was halfway back to his car. She watched him go, but he didn't look back. She felt like she'd been punched in the chest.

"What a rude, contentious bastard!" Sophia retorted, watching him leave.

He's not! Elsa wanted to scream after her! *He's really, bloody not!* It was she who had messed up. But hey, whose side was she meant to be on?

"So, what was all that about anyway?" Sophia asked her, as they walked back to the lorry, away from any prying ears of the stabling area.

"I bashed into him as I went flying around the corner," Elsa murmured, pulling her cardigan guardedly around her, her eyes never leaving the ground. "But I said sorry. Don't know what his problem was."

"Oh well. You look stunning by the way, where have you been?" Sophia tried again, accepting her plausible story.

"Just out for dinner with an old friend who lives nearby," Elsa replied feebly with a shrug.

"Frederick Twemlow looked like he'd been out somewhere nice, too." Sophia sighed, thinking how he always dressed as though he were about to go somewhere nice and luxurious.

"I didn't speak to him long enough to ask," Elsa looked up, held her gaze. "I bumped into him on my way into the barn, nearly sent him flying. Hence he wasn't very happy with me."

"You can say that again," Sophia retorted, her eyebrows raised. "So, tell me about your dinner? An old male friend, by any chance?"

"Possibly."

They climbed up into the lorry. Elsa quickly peeled off her dress, as delightful as it was she just wanted to be out of it and in her fleecy pyjamas, tucked up in bed with the only boy that should matter to her. She had everything she'd ever wanted, right here – so why did she suddenly feel so sad? Why did she feel so empty, like something was missing?

"Boyfriend material?" Sophia smiled.

"Very unlikely." Elsa concentrated on neatly folding the dress, avoiding eye contact.

"You obviously thought enough of him to go out of your way for dinner with him."

"Not really." She shrugged, holding Cecil close and pulling her duvet around the both of them. "He lives nearby, thought I might as well while I was in the area."

"Isn't it about time you found a nice boyfriend?" Sophia murmured, searching through the cupboards for anything edible. "Horses can't keep you warm at night."

"You sound just like your mother." Elsa sighed, not really in the mood for this conversation right now.

"Oh, has she been on at you as well? Try living with her, I get it every day. I think she's hoping someone with a nice big house and stable yard will take me on and marry me, get me out from under her feet." She paused.

Elsa suddenly sat up in amusement. "So, when are you going to put that poor, bloody vet out of his misery?"

Sophia spun round, and Elsa cheered up now that the tables were turned.

"I've no idea what you're talking about," Sophia muttered, blushing.

"Oh, give over!" Elsa laughed. "He fancies you something rotten, and you him."

"No, I do not!" she exclaimed, but her voice was far from convincing. She appeared to give it some thought. "Do you really think he does?" she asked eventually.

"A blind man could see that he does," Elsa rolled her eyes. "How are you so oblivious? He's been dying to ask you out for ages but he's so *shy*. I'm getting fed up with it – one of you needs to make the first move! Looks like he'll be dead before it's him."

"Oh God, no I can't," she looked bewildered. "You might have got the wrong end of the stick and he'll turn me down and I might not ever be able to look at him again. And he's a bloody good vet."

"You never look at him anyway," Elsa pointed out. "But maybe you should; he's quite a catch is Harry. I wouldn't kick him out of bed."

"Elsa! Please stop!" Sophia implored, her cheeks now crimson. "Your new friend Ava appears to be a bad influence on you and has obviously been leading you astray, I'll have to have words with her! Although I admire her, how on earth does she get any work done for Frederick Twemlow? I'd be *so* distracted..." she let out a sigh and slumped down on the bench seat that separated the living area from the lorry cab.

"He's so dreamy, isn't he? I wish I could impress Frederick-bloody-Twemlow. Do you think he'd let me share his lorry? I bet his fridge is better stocked than ours."

"Why? I wouldn't want to impress him." Elsa cut her off. "Plus, there's more to life than money."

"Everyone says that, but look at him – people can't help it. Look at his horses, and his yard. You certainly made some sort of impression on him – it didn't look too good, though."

"Thanks," Elsa mumbled sulkily, although she wasn't sure Sophia heard.

"Here," Sophia sat up, a thought suddenly occurring. "He wasn't poaching you for the job, was he? I hear he's employing...*again*. I bet he's an arse to work for."

"No, he wasn't," Elsa quickly put her mind at rest.

Elsa rolled over to face the wall. Cecil yawned and stretched out alongside her. She'd had enough for one day. She tried not to make a sound as an involuntary tear ran down her cheek, no doubt taking her makeup with it. The last thing she wanted was Sophia seeing her upset and asking her what was wrong. She had never wanted to be that person that cried over a guy; she'd always thought she was stronger than that. But she just couldn't help it.

She pulled her pillow closer to muffle any escaping sobs. *What the fuck had she done?* But she knew she only had herself to blame. The most eligible bachelor in the equine world wanted to get to know her, and she had pretty much told him to shove off. All she'd wanted was to be certain that if she found a guy she liked, that he couldn't make her sad, yet he'd failed that one already, so now why was she the one feeling bad? *And I'm not crying over a guy*, she told herself, before slowly succumbing to sleep. *I'm crying at myself because I'm a helpless idiot.*

Elsa rolled over and stretched out. The window curtain caught in her duvet, flooding the lorry with early morning light. Cecil yelped and jumped out of the way, and she suddenly had a clear recollection of her horrendous night before. She grabbed Cecil and pulled him back to her chest, and she was quickly forgiven with a lick to the face.

She pulled on her shorts and t-shirt, grabbed a pack of baby wipes from her emergency grooming box, and set about wiping the smudged makeup from her face. Her alarm hadn't gone off yet, and Sophia was still sleeping, but Cecil was already waiting at the door. She might as well go and feed the horses. The weather looked promising; maybe she'd stand under the hose with Merlin while she bathed him.

The horses kicked at their stall doors as soon as they saw her enter the barn. Grooms were already there; but luckily Sophia hadn't drawn a really early slot.

"Hey!" came a booming voice, and footsteps ran up behind her. "So... tell me how your hot date went – are you hungover from a night of passion?"

"I already told you, it wasn't a hot date," Elsa told the excited Australian.

"Did he like the dress?" Ava implored, hands on hips. That dress had always worked for her.

"I think he *loved* the dress." Elsa admitted, her cheeks flushing as she remembered all the times Frederick had told her she was beautiful.

"And are you going to see him again?" Ava probed.

Elsa bit her lip. After the way they had left things? She had blown it. Slowly and reluctantly she shook her head. "No, I don't think so."

"Ah, shame!" Ava gently shook her shoulder. "I had high hopes for you and this mystery man of yours, but there's plenty more fish in the sea!"

"Too right," Elsa forced a smile. *Pull yourself together!* She bossily told herself.

Merlin banged impatiently at his door, annoyed that his groom was gossiping when he was still to be fed.

"Alright, I'm on it!" Elsa told him, scratching the gelding's nose and quickly removing her hand before he tried to nip her fingers.

"Have you seen Frederick about this morning?" Ava asked casually, frowning. "He was in a right strop when he came back last night, and he was out well before me this morning."

"No, sorry," Elsa replied, thoughtful. Surely she couldn't be talking about Mr Cool. *Had she affected him that much?*

Merlin was happy to be back out at an event, and pulled Elsa down to the warm up ring. She rode him around for ten minutes before legging Sophia up on-board, and left her in the hands of Derek while she went to find herself an ice-cold drink.

A final sponge around the face, a splash of hoof oil on his black hooves, and she waved them off into the ring.

She saw him across the ring; sitting astride a huge bay as it crossed the warm up in a glorious extended canter. He sat so gently, so light, his long, perfect legs wrapped around the bays side. She just wished he'd look up and notice her, maybe give her just another chance even though she'd had so many already. But he was so focused on the job in hand; he didn't look like he carried any of the traumas that she was feeling of her lost opportunity to wake up beside him this morning. Even if realistically that could never have happened; just to feel his soft lips brush against hers would have been enough, a promise of more to come.

The shrill ring of the start bell brought her back to her senses. She quickly shoved Merlin's sweatsheet and bandages back into her rucksack, and sprinted to the ring side just as Sophia started her test.

Elsa could see Merlin maturing with every event they brought him to, and he was relishing performing in front of larger crowds than he was previously used to. Whilst some of their transitions were still a bit sticky, and he had the occasional concentration lapse, he did a pleasing enough test to land her in fifteenth place in a big class.

Elsa was waiting with his sugar lumps when he came out, and jumped on him to get him cooled and back to the barn to get him ready for the show jumping, while Sophia debriefed with Derek.

She quickly sponged him off, gave him another brush, and left him with some hay before it was time to change him into his jumping tack. While she chatted with her neighbouring grooms, she knew from Ava that Frederick was busy with three rides today and had started early, and would be out on cross country while Sophia was show jumping, so there was minimum chance of her bumping into him.

Sophia and Merlin's grid work practice at home under Derek's watchful eye had obviously been paying off, as he had only one pole in the show jumping, when Sophia realised she was down on the time and turned too tight into a big oxer to try and compensate, and Merlin just could not make it despite trying with all his might.

Rosie appeared, sloshing the wine in her glass as she thrust it into her husband's hands and threw her arms around Merlin.

"Oh, he's such a *good boy*!" she squealed, smothering him in kisses. "Do be good across country, won't you?"

Elsa smiled, waiting until Ernie had had enough and removed his enthusiastic wife from the embarrassed-looking gelding, returned her the wine glass, before leading the gelding away.

Elsa rested him before the cross country, walked Cecil and held Ruby and Connor out for a pick of grass. They had been wondering why today wasn't about them. She packed some of the dressage kit into the lorry and tidied the stalls. She wanted to get out of here as soon as possible; Picton hadn't been a particularly enjoyable outing for her this time, although an improvement on their previous trip to Napier.

Merlin was raring to go as Sophia headed for the start box. She started her watch, and they were off. All Elsa could do was wait; sweatsheet folded over her arms.

There was no rain this week, which meant reduced fears of Merlin slipping. He loved the ground and handled it well. He stormed round well within the time, even though Sophia had taken the easier, longer combination at one of the fences where she'd feared he wouldn't have enough space. He clearly loved the bigger fences and a more challenging track.

"He's a smashing little horse!" Ava mentioned, as Elsa passed her on her way back to the barn.

"You can eye this one up as much as you like!" Elsa told her. "Sophia owns half of him, so he won't be going anywhere!"

"I told you, we've got enough horses!" Ava laughed. "But do have a serious think about that job offer!"

Elsa replied with just a smile, and was out of earshot. Work for Frederick Twemlow? As if she'd ever seriously thought about it, but there was no way she would now. She was still so angry at herself, and so angry at him. She wanted to stay as far away as possible to save herself from embarrassing herself anymore in his presence with her supposed moral high ground. At least that was what she could try and tell herself.

"Picton," she murmured later that afternoon, as she waved a thank you and goodbye to the official stopping the cars for her to exit the lorry park. "The course of so many opportunities that I well and truly fucked up."

Still, at least her horses had performed well. No rosettes this weekend, but they had tried their hearts out and been just outside the placings, and Sophia was bound to get noticed by owners soon. The drive home would be a jovial one.

With a lull in Sophia's event schedule while her horses had a break, Elsa had more time to prepare Bear. She took her hacking out across the hills to help build up her muscle and improve her stamina, and give her some confidence being alone. She was used to being ridden out in a string of horses when in race training, and in her early days with Elsa had refused to go anywhere alone, but now they had mostly conquered that.

Two days before their event, Elsa took Bear for a blast along a local racehorse trainer's gallops, which confirmed to Elsa she had all the speed and brakes that she needed. The day before she had a gentle schooling session and popped a couple of small, easy jumps in the paddock destined to build their confidence rather than challenge them at this late stage.

The evening before, she had cleaned her tack until it was sparkling, bathed her pony, and settled for an early night to try and put her nerves at bay.

Elsa always travelled to her own competitions alone. She was used to the multi-tasking of getting several horses ready at once, and so only having just herself and one horse to worry about had never troubled her.

Bear was more of a drama queen than any of Sophia's horses though, and Elsa had seen over the last few months that when the local racehorse trainer had mentioned one night in the pub that he was having trouble rehoming a particular mare and Elsa had straight away agreed to have her – why others who knew the mare may have been more reluctant to take her on.

Bear was kicking the lorry as soon as Elsa pulled to a halt in the lorry park, and whinnying to be let off. Elsa peered through the groom's door and gave her a slice of carrot, then left her to it while she went to get booked in.

Elsa had learned during their very first outing that Bear did not like to be tied to the lorry, and so she tacked her up and got her ready as best she could while she was still on the lorry, and often asked a passer-by to kindly hold her once outside so that she could put studs in and check her tack in daylight. If there was going to be a long wait between sections, or Elsa needed to walk the course, she would load her back up, and Bear seemed happy with this, so long as she had a bulging haynet.

Elsa had not reached the sophisticated heights of Sophia's eventing that required different tack for different phases, so there was no tack changing required between sections. Elsa had had enough trouble finding even one saddle that fit the odd shaped mare, and her grooms wage could not stretch to a dressage saddle, so she did all three disciplines in her jump saddle. At the snail's pace that their progress was going, she couldn't imagine needing a dressage saddle any time soon.

Dressage was definitely Bear's weakest phase, and the quirky mare detested having Elsa's legs too far down her sides, so Elsa often went into competition with much shorter stirrups than her competitors. The last time Elsa had tried letting her stirrups down to dressage length, Bear had disagreed so much that she had launched Elsa across the arena and she'd landed on her rear right in front of the judge's car. It had been a problem that Elsa had tried to rectify at home, but had just found in the end that Bear much preferred to have her rider sitting perched like a flat jockey, and as Sophia's busy schedule meant that Elsa and Bear had minimal opportunity for outings, Elsa was happy to put up with shorter than usual stirrups for the time being. She had little concern for what the minimal spectators thought of her unorthodox style.

Bear was on fire in the warm up, and the little, chestnut mare definitely lived up to her feisty stereotype as she hauled Elsa around. She had not changed much by the time it came to her test. The working trot was a little over-enthusiastic, she tossed her head and tried to run on into canter, and Elsa tried anything she could think of to distract the rebellious mare from her wayward thoughts and keep her mind on the job at hand. She nailed the twenty metre circles with the perfect bend and rhythm, and although her transitions were a little sketchy, she hit all the markers perfectly with her changes of rein. She eventually settled enough to pull off a decent enough test. It left lots of things for Elsa to work on at home, if only she could ever find the time.

She dismounted and walked the enthusiastic mare back to the lorry. Bear knew what was coming next, and was already on her toes. It was a grey day and a drizzle lingered in the air. Elsa pulled her coat around her, trying not to get too cold while she waited.

The lorry ramp was down, and she sat on the edge, her arm linked through Bear's reins while they both had a drink and something to eat. Bear nuzzled her pockets, ever hopeful for carrots, and Elsa tore the crusts from her sandwich for Cecil, not wanting to have favourites. She was aware of a small commotion across the lorry park; she heard an excited shout a couple of lorry's away, and saw the group next door swatting each other on the arms and pointing, and Elsa followed their gaze with a frown.

And then she saw him, strolling through the lorry park. He ran his hand through his thick, blond hair; scanning the lorries and faces as if looking for someone, totally oblivious to the attention he was attracting; the disbelieving stares of admiration. *He was here.* Elsa was on her feet, fumbling with her girths. Her show jumping wasn't for a while yet, but he was heading straight at her and she needed to get out of here before he saw her. He wouldn't want to see her; it would be too awkward and embarrassing.

Cecil had seen him too and barked, his hackles raised.

"In the lorry, fella," Elsa told him. "Now!"

But he refused, and when she turned back to look at Frederick, her eyes could barely leave him. Bear fidgeted as Elsa fumbled blindly with her girths.

He looked up, caught her eye, and a smile immediately lit up his face.

"Elsa! There you are!" He hurried to her, releasing his hands from the pockets of his beige corduroys, his checked shirt unbuttoned at the top.

Her eyes widened. She stopped fumbling with the girth straps, her hands suddenly shaking. *There you are? Was he actually looking for her?*

"Here I am," she shrugged. "What are you doing here?"

"It's a horse trials, Elsa. That's where I normally hang out." An amused smile tugged at the corners of those perfect lips.

"Yea, I know, but..." she shrugged. Wasn't this a bit lowly for him? "I thought you had a clinic today?"

"Have you been keeping tabs on me?" he smiled.

"No!" she said quickly, her cheeks reddening. But Sophia had mentioned it in the week, and Elsa had wished she could have had the nerve to take Bear along, and the money, of course. But groom's wages certainly did not stretch to clinics with the one-and-only *Frederick Twemlow.*

"I'm teasing you," he said gently. "I finished early. Pretty little pony you have there."

"Thanks. This is Timber Bear." Elsa introduced her proudly.

"Timber Bear?" he repeated, eyebrows raised as he now failed to conceal his amusement. "Elsa, are you serious?"

"Yes, I'm serious! Don't offend her – she's already a little fresh."

"How was your dressage?" He asked kindly, giving Bear a friendly pat as he silently but knowingly assessed her. "I assume you've already been?"

She nodded, following his gaze flicker over her pony. "Strained. I really struggled to keep her soft and listening to me. We'll probably have all the show jumps down, and if we even get half way round the cross country it'll be miracle."

"Maybe I can help?" he suggested.

Her breath caught in surprise. "You can? Well, of course, if anyone can then it's you, but... do you have time? Do you not have a pupil you've come to help or something?" She looked around, as if expecting someone to join him at any moment.

"No," he grinned. "I do the occasional clinic, Elsa, but I don't have time to have any *pupils.* So here I am, at your disposal."

She didn't quite know what to say. She just stared at him in horror. "Oh, good God." She murmured eventually, realising he was being serious. "No pressure then?"

"None," he said gently. "Actually, Elsa, I've been desperate to see you."

"You have?" she felt her heart racing.

He nodded, and sat down on the ramp. She felt obliged to sit down beside him, her arm slipped through Bear's reins and totally oblivious to the curious stares she was receiving from the neighbouring lorries. Their arms were almost touching, and she suddenly wished that despite the chill, she didn't have her jacket on.

"In my haste of trying to prove to you that I am not in fact a prick, it appears I behaved a lot like a prick." He told her humbly.

"Oh, I didn't notice," she mumbled.

He gave a gentle laugh, and looked right at her. She felt her heart beating in her mouth. His soft lips were just inches away, and they still looked so kissable. Heat radiated from him, and he sat so close that her whole body was in turmoil.

"Excuse me," came a small voice.

They both spun, flustered, to see a teenager before them, poised with pen and paper in hand.

She gave an apologetic shrug. "Please can I have your autograph?"

"Of course," Frederick smiled, getting to his feet, he took the pen and paper from her. "What is your name?"

"Anna," she beamed proudly, and Elsa could have sworn she was fluttering her eyelashes at him.

Anna, he scribbled. *Best wishes, Frederick Twemlow.*

She took it from him with a look of pure joy, kissed the paper and jubilantly jumped up and down, which sent Bear recoiling in horror.

"Do you compete?" he asked her kindly, as Elsa calmed her pony.

"Yes," she nodded eagerly. "I have a warmblood, he's not here today, but hopefully one day we'll be competing against you." She gave a nervous laugh.

Frederick smiled. "I'm sure you will." He told her, and watched her run off excitedly back to her friends. Elsa watched them high five each other in glee.

"Do you get this everywhere horsey that you go?" Elsa asked him.

"Not jealous, are we?" his gorgeous blue eyes implored her.

"Not one bit," she lied, breaking contact.

"So, when are you jumping?" he got to his feet. "Is it time to warm up? Let me be your groom for the day?"

She held back her laugh. She did her girths up with less fumbling, and let Frederick leg her up into the saddle, even though she could mount easily from the lorry ramp, any touch from him was a bonus.

They walked down to the warm up side-by-side, and Elsa couldn't believe how relaxed and carefree he seemed. And while Elsa normally had to fight for space in the generally crowded warm up arenas, people just moved out of the way and stopped in awe to see Frederick Twemlow in the flesh. *Here, at Nelson.* She looked in amusement at the star struck faces around her, as he instructed her, totally oblivious to all the attention he was receiving.

"Push her on," he told her. "She's got bundles of energy, so *use it* don't restrain it."

Elsa wasn't sure if she rode better or worse with his eyes constantly fixed on her, but it seemed to be working. Bear was a lot more responsive and a lot less argumentative. Normally Elsa didn't have much chance of a practice jump; she had no one to help adjust the heights and replace any falling poles, but Frederick cleared the way, put up a gentle cross pole and called her into it. No one cut her up like they usually did; her way was cleared. No one would dare get in the way of Frederick Twemlow and his exceedingly lucky pupil.

"Leg, *leg!*" he roared, taking Elsa by surprise. "She wants to go, hold her and push her and she'll jump with a much better shape."

Elsa did as he said, gave her a check a few strides out and then made sure her leg was firmly on to prevent her from backing off. Bear cleared it exuberantly and Elsa gave her a grateful pat.

"Much better," Frederick commented. "Don't be afraid to let her go a bit Elsa. Don't do anything with your hands unless you're going to back it up with your leg."

She walked her off and it was her time to go in. Quite a crowd had accumulated to determine what was so special about Elsa and this ordinary, rather naughty chestnut mare that they obtained Frederick's undivided attention, and Elsa couldn't help but be nervous with the extra eyes upon her.

The bell rang and Elsa nodded at the judge and pushed her little mare from walk to a perfect canter. She gave the over excited mare a half halt, and immediately put her leg on when she felt her back off. She already felt more rounded as they turned for the first fence, and she flew over it.

The real battle began half way round, when Bear's confidence had grown enough that she felt she could do this on her own now, and Elsa was just a hindrance. Her head was coming back up, and Elsa struggled to hold her. She had the last part of the combination down and ran on too fast to the upright planks. Elsa couldn't check her in time, and she took that out as well, but had enough control to fly the last.

"Good," Frederick said simply as she exited the ring. "She definitely looks a handful, but you must let go of her. While you're hanging onto her you're just a dead weight on the end of her rein."

"I know that," Elsa replied breathlessly. "It's just..." she broke off helplessly, realising it would take a lot to get the approval of such a perfectionist. And who was she to argue with *him*?

"Give and take, Elsa," he told her, holding her gaze. "It's all about give and take." And as she watched him she wondered if he was still talking about Bear.

She slid from the saddle, and his arm was around her back as she met the floor. She tried to hide her surprise, but his touch felt *so* good, even through all these clothes.

"Are you sure you've got enough brakes for the cross country?" he asked her, genuinely concerned.

"I normally do," she shrugged. "We've never actually made it all the way round before, though."

"And why's that?" he asked from under raised eyebrows.

She felt like a scolded child. "We had a lot of napping issues when I first got her. Normally she takes offence to a particular jump half way round and throws in the towel."

"Well, if that happens today, what are you going to do?" he crossed his arms across his chest. *Oh, how she longed to peel that shirt off him and trail her fingers across that chest. Maybe even her lips...*

She shrugged. "Probably tense up, ride like the awful rider I really am and tell myself to stick to grooming?"

He ignored her. "I've no room for negativity in my life, Elsa. You'll drop your reins, put your leg on, and back it up with your stick if necessary. You'll do anything to get her going forward, and then praise her. If you need to retire her, you retire her when she is happy and moving forward. Even if you get disqualified, don't worry, give her a pat and then you bring her around to mine in the week and we'll school her over my fences."

He was looking right at her. She didn't know what to say. "Have you just invited me over?" she eventually asked.

"I may just have done." He smiled. "I guess I'll know whether you really want to come or not, by whether you get disqualified."

"I've no room for that kind of negativity in my life," she told him, swinging herself back into the saddle easily from the horsebox ramp. "I'm riding for a clear."

"That's my girl!" he smiled, then paused. "I wanted to help you into the saddle," he told her with a frown. "I thought you needed me?"

"Oh, I do," she leaned down so she was just inches from him. "You can help me find my stirrups, if you want?" And she thrust her calf into his waiting palm.

He shook his head with a grin as he held her calf for a moment before placing her toe in the stirrup irons. She was surprised at her own brazenness, and her heart was beating over time as she realised their past awkward meeting seemed to have been forgotten.

The starter called her in, and just when she thought Bear might start to nap, she relaxed her hand and dug her heels in deep and they were off.

Had he called her his girl? She was pretty sure he had, even if it was just a turn of phrase. Surely it could have some meaning? What were the consequences of being referred to as someone's *girl*?

The first fence neared, and Elsa gathered her little mare up and cleared the flower beds easily. And he had invited her over, too. She wondered whether he ever invited anyone to school over his fences, she'd never heard of anything of the sort from Sophia or Ava. Was he just genuinely being nice, because he was nice to anyone?

She spun around the corner, and upon the ditch. She pushed Bear on to meet the stride, but Bear saw a long one and Elsa tried her utmost not to get left behind.

"Concentrate, Elsa!" she scolded herself, and Bear twitched her ears to listen. "Not you, darling," Elsa told her. "You're doing fab!"

Up the slight hill, and Elsa met the brush fence double. She needed three long strides in-between, and she got them perfectly.

The course was straightforward and the jumps welcoming, one of the main reasons Elsa had chosen it for her first competition back after a few reluctant weeks off. It would not be challenging to a seasoned competitor, but Bear was a former steeplechaser, and while her semi-illustrious career had proved she could gallop and jump hedges, occasionally the more creative cross-country fences had her stumped. This week she was travelling well until the picnic table, and she slammed on the brakes.

Elsa wasn't sure what exactly it was about the picnic table that Bear decided she didn't like, or whether it was nothing in particular apart from deciding she'd quite like to go back to the lorry now, but her determination not to humiliate herself in front of Frederick set in.

"*Get on!*" she growled, and brought her stick down on the mare's flank, who responded with a fly-buck. She relaxed her hands and dug her heels in, but Bear spun quickly and kicked out, almost throwing her off balance. But Elsa was wise to this trick, and she spun her back and kicked harder.

With a buck and a snort, Bear lurched forward and decided she would clear the picnic table after all, but about three feet higher than necessary and in a style somewhat representing a stag.

"Good girl!" Elsa patted her sweaty neck profusely as she pushed her on. They had lost precious time, but it didn't matter. Just knowing that Frederick was there, *watching her*, was already making her ride better, and Bear felt her new sense of determination.

They flew the coffin, and then onto another simple ditch. Elsa shuddered mid-air; for she still had nightmares about the first time Bear had deposited her at the bottom of one. She steadied her for the corner jump, and then there was a tight turn that took her through a wooded area, and over a simple roll-top which was on a downhill slope.

The last fence was another brush, and Elsa knew this would pose no problems for Bear.

"This is the best day *ever!*" she squealed upon landing, and galloped to the finish, absolutely elated.

Chapter Nine

Frederick was waiting for her, having managed to detract himself from the crowd that was trying to attach to him. He didn't try to hide his relief that she was back. He took the little mares rein as Elsa slowed to a walk beside him, and gave her a hearty pat as they both recovered their breathing.

"You'd make a good groom," Elsa teased, as she recovered her breath. "Did you bring the sweatsheet, too?"

"Don't push your luck." He paused, and turned to look at her. "You're not a bad jockey either, are you?"

She shrugged and twisted a clump of Bear's loose mane distractedly through her fingers.

"You did well." He told her sincerely. "She looked tricky."

"She is." Elsa nodded, meeting his gaze.

"I suppose the best girls are," he said, not taking his eyes from her.

She felt her cheeks reddening, and her stomach flipped a somersault. *How did he do this to her?*

"I'll let you walk her off for me, if you think you're good enough?" She smiled. "I am dying for a drink."

Smiling, he pulled a chilled bottle of water from his coat and passed it to her. "I'm not *that* good, Elsa, but Ava would be sacked if I ever finished my round and she wasn't waiting there with water – both for me and the horse. Thought I'd better practice what I preach."

Elsa laughed, and took a long, grateful sip. However, her groom's clear path to the lorry park was suddenly blocked by another teen poised with pen and a napkin.

"Please," the teen smiled, nervously. "Can I have your autograph?"

"Of course," Frederick obliged. As she scuttled off to show

her friends, he turned to Elsa. "Please get down from that horse and let me cool her off? They can't get to me up there."

Laughing, Elsa slid from the saddle and legged him up.

Cecil barked upon their return to the lorry. He did not look best pleased to see Frederick up on his horse.

He dismounted, and Elsa began stripping her tack off and washing her down.

"I'm afraid I'm not so good at this bit," Frederick told her, stepping aside.

"That's fine, because I am. Make yourself useful and pour me a tea from my flask."

As he reached inside the groom's door, Cecil barked, hackles raised.

"Your dog really doesn't like me." He called nervously over his shoulder.

"Leave him, Cecil!" Elsa said sharply, and he whined and went back to his bed.

"So, no ribbon for today, but you didn't put on a bad show," Frederick passed her a plastic cup of tea.

"I bet if that had been your performance today, you'd be furious with how you'd done?" she asked him.

"Depends if I'd learned anything from it. The end result is irrelevant; it's what we take away from the experience that counts."

"Every day's a school day, huh?" She slipped Bear a sugar cube.

"Too right," he smiled. "Well done, she looks like a tricky mare, and you get on very well with her. I think you'll go far together."

"Thanks," she smiled, feeling immensely proud. "That means a lot."

He was looking at her so intently, and she didn't ever want to peel her eyes away from him. She wondered what he was doing here – like *really* doing here. With her. But she could wonder all she liked, for she didn't feel he would tell her any time soon, and she busied herself with Bear's travel boots, while Frederick bandaged her tail.

Despite Bear's utmost refusal to stand still for them, she was eventually ready to head home, and Elsa boxed her up without any drama, and she dived happily into her haynet.

"Ready?" Frederick forced a smile, not wanting to leave her. He'd had the best afternoon; he wished they could do this more often.

"Actually, I'm just going to go and have a look at the professional photos," Elsa hopped from foot to foot, suddenly feeling embarrassed and wondering if he was in a hurry to get away.

"Of course!" he looked delighted. "Lead the way."

"Sorry, which one were you?" the young photographer asked, barely able to peel her eyes from Frederick.

"Number sixty-eight," Elsa replied for the second time, keeping her tongue firmly bitten. She may as well not be there at all, the photographer had not looked at her once.

She was barely listening as she nodded and fluttered her eyelashes at Frederick, who did his best not to notice.

"A little chestnut mare," Elsa added helpfully. "She had bright blue boots on."

She sensed Frederick roll his eyes at her colour choice, and felt her cheeks flushing, but was quickly distracted as a photo of her and Timber Bear sideways on, clearing the coffin in style flashed up on the photographer's laptop, and Elsa clasped her hands together in glee.

"Ah, doesn't she look fab!" she couldn't help herself. Bear had her legs snapped up tight, looking as though she could have done with the jump being twice the height.

"We got you at the open ditch, too," the photographer flicked to the next photo, to show Elsa and Bear head on, the concentration across both of their faces evident.

"There's a dressage one," she went on, and the screen showed Elsa performing a less than perfect working trot, desperately trying to hold it together, and Timber Bear looking like she had four left hooves.

"And the show jumping," the screen flashed again to show Elsa and Bear in perfect unison across a bright yellow and black spread, the little mare's ears pricked forward.

"Which one shall I get?" she turned to Frederick.

"Get them all," Frederick grinned, equally delighted at them all.

Elsa forced a smile, scratching her head. At fifteen pounds for a printed photo, her groom's wages didn't stretch to buying more than one, as much as she'd love to.

"I'll take the first one, please," Elsa told her, biting her bottom lip. The second one was lovely too....*no*, she told herself. *You can't afford it – be strong.*

She nodded defiantly. "Yes, the coffin, please."

"Don't be silly," Frederick laughed, taking his wallet from his pocket. "She'll have them all, my treat."

"No, you can't do that!" her eyes widened, but he had already passed the photographer his card, and she did not look like she would ever deny him.

"Of course I can." He gave her a wink, and she felt herself blushing and knew she would not argue with him.

He placed his arm protectively around her, and she watched the photographer shrink away with his card and a scowl. *This really is the best day ever!* Elsa thought, never wanting him to remove his hand from her hip.

Photo's duly printed, Elsa clasped them in delight, and they made their way back to the lorry for the final time. Elsa had been dreading this bit all afternoon; the time they must go their separate ways.

"I can't ever thank you enough for today," she said gently, hesitating. "For your help."

"It was nothing," he shrugged, and reached forward, tenderly touching her arm. "But hopefully makes up a little for my behaviour the other night?" He hesitated. He desperately wanted to kiss her, but he feared it was too soon. He wasn't sure if he was forgiven yet.

"It's not nothing." Elsa breathed, staying deadly still and praying he would not move away from her. "I do all of this alone, it means a lot to have a bit of company, especially as you probably have a million more important things to do."

"Not really," he whispered, his glorious blue eyes baring into her.

"I would like to say thank you properly." She went on, while she was feeling brave. "For today and for the lovely dinner last week, which I rudely barely touched. How about I cook you dinner tonight?"

"I can't," he sighed, stepping away in frustration as he remembered his prior commitment.

"Oh," her face fell, but she quickly forced a smile, and defiantly crossed her arms across her chest.

"No, I would love to," he insisted, noticing her disappointment. "It's not an excuse – but I really can't tonight – I've got a family thing that I can't get out of." Oh, how he wished he could get out of it; he could think of many things he'd rather be doing with her, instead.

"That's OK," she shrugged. "Well, thanks for the photos anyway. Guess I need to add that to my list of things to thank you for."

"I'll call you," he promised, and just when she thought he might finally kiss her, he was gone, striding through the lorry park like a man on a mission, before anyone had a chance to notice and leach onto him.

She watched him until he was out of sight, and let out a huge sigh. Her body slumped and she hugged herself tightly; her mind just a big muddle. It had been a long day, and Elsa couldn't wait to get back to her home comforts, her pyjamas and a glass of wine so that she could sit down and try and process all these thoughts that were jumbling her mind.

Frederick had to get out of here, away from the

disappointment at himself that she finally wanted to share dinner with him, and it was him turning her down. But he had *promised* his mother that he and Ava would attend this party; the Roxwell's were coming and they did support him generously with horse power. But he could make it up to them by taking them out to dinner on another night. They were understanding people, and although Frederick supposed Elsa was too, she was surely more important? He paused just before he reached the Range Rover, and ploughed his fingers through his hair. Would his mother be disappointed if he bowed out of her event? Heck, she was disappointed at him with whatever decision he made in life, wasn't she?

Elsa wasn't sure to feel elated or heavily disappointed as she swung the lorry out onto the road. Of course, she was elated for so many reasons; she and Bear had put in their best performance to date, and Frederick had spent most of the day with her. He had made it quite clear he had gone there just for her; he had remembered from dinner that she was competing. He had focused solely on her the whole time. It had been he who had *made* her get around. So why should she feel disappointed? Last week she had been so close to a kiss one minute; to thinking she may never see him again in the next breath. Today he had seemed so *disinterested* in rekindling their tender moment.

"And they say girls are confusing?" she growled at Cecil, curled up on the passenger seat. She slammed her fists on the steering wheel, and his dark eyes regarded her with suspicion. "I am so confused right now."

He yawned and resumed his nap. She turned up the radio, and switched channels until she found an emotional break up ballad that made her want to cry.

"This is how I'm feeling right now, OK?" she retaliated to Cecil's protests, but she couldn't help feeling that her loyal companion and his hackles would be more than happy if they never laid eyes on Frederick Twemlow again.

Elsa pulled her towel tighter around her and sat down in the tatty, comfy armchair. She took her first sip of cold, white wine, and didn't realise until it hit the back of her throat how much she needed it. Sweet, tangy and refreshing, she let out the deepest of sighs and took another sip.

Her stomach rumbled; she hadn't eaten since breakfast. She knew she should eat, and she knew the perils of drinking on an empty stomach, but the wine tasted so good and her muscles ached so much she wasn't sure if they'd allow her to stand up again and fight her way to the kitchen now that they'd found solace in the armchair.

Cecil whined, reminding her that he hadn't eaten, either.

"I'm sorry, fella," she put the wine glass down and opened her arms to him. "Cuddle first, food later?"

Ever obliging, he hauled his gangly frame up onto her lap, and tried his best to curl up. At least all the horses on the yard had been hayed and watered, and she didn't need to go out again. She had headed straight for a long, glorious shower, and could think of nothing better to round off the night than snuggle with her mutt in front of a shitty film.

"What would I do without you to welcome me home every night, huh?" she murmured, rubbing his favourite soft spot behind his long, shabby ears.

His head spun around to attention, and he barked, and she groaned and waited for the impending ring of the doorbell. She considered staying put, and continuing to let her aching legs rest. It was followed by a gentle knock, not an urgent hammering that immediately required her attention, like if Sophia had an emergency with one of the horses. She waited for them to get bored and leave her be, but Cecil had already jumped to the floor and upped his guard dog campaign, and her stomach rumbled so loudly that she fleetingly wondered if maybe Petra had brought her dinner after all. Ever hopeful, she dragged herself up and followed Cecil out into the tiny hallway. Remembering how very naked she was underneath her towel, she pulled open the door just a fraction, and her cheery smile immediately turned to a gasp.

He looked *beautiful*. He wore a crisp blue shirt, with the top two buttons undone. His jeans hung perfectly on his slender frame, his ruffled blonde curls swept back from his face. That wonderful, chiselled jaw, those wholly kissable lips...

"I thought you were out for a moment," he said quietly, trying to keep the nerves at bay as his soft blue eyes drank in the image of her. He hoped she wanted to see him, and didn't want to intrude. She obviously wasn't dressed for visitors, he noticed with amusement, and was even more determined that she'd let him in.

Her eyebrows rose. She scraped back her hair; and dreaded to think what she must look like. She prayed that the long shower had done its job and she no longer had any straw poking out of her hair, or mud smeared across her face.

"How did you know where I lived?" she breathed.

"This is Sophia's yard," he glanced over his shoulder as if to double check, amused. "This is a groom's cottage, and you are her groom. I kind of put two and two together."

"Of course," she felt her cheeks reddening. His bright blue eyes searched hers. She suddenly felt so self-conscious, and she hugged her towel tighter around her.

"Shit, sorry," he mumbled, suddenly backing away. "I shouldn't have intruded. I'll go."

What? No! She tried to hide her panic as she opened the door wider. "Please, come in."

"You're sure?" His eyebrows rose.

"Yes, of course," she stood back so he could enter and closed the door behind him. She hesitated. "But I haven't cooked dinner. I know I said I would, but you said you were busy."

"I was...I am. It wasn't a lie." He ran his hand over his soft stubble. "It was a family thing. I couldn't get out of it. But...well, Ava was there – my Mother invites her to everything – and I had to get away."

"Oh?" her breath caught. She felt her heart quicken. *Was there something going on between him and Ava?*

In the end, he'd just slipped out without a word; they were probably all wondering where he was right now. But Ava could look after the owners for him, because this was much more important – there was something he had to get off his chest and it would not wait.

"Oh, shit. This isn't easy," he began, hesitating in the tiny hallway, aware of how close his body was to hers. "But Ava keeps talking about you, and how you'd be a good fit for the job we're advertising. She tells me she's been trying to poach you."

"She has tried, yes." Elsa replied, guarded. She was unsure of where this was going and whether she'd like it.

"We really do need someone spectacular. But I don't want you to apply." He implored, reaching for her arm. "I don't want you to be disappointed and I want to save you from any hurt. Please, don't apply for the job."

"Hmm?" She felt the colour drain from her face, not moving away from his grip. What had he heard about her? She ran a tight ship at home, and away at events, Sophia's horses were turned out to the highest standard. *She'd won the bloody Turnbridge cup, for goodness sake!*

"Because if you applied, then I'd accept because you do an impeccable job of grooming," he breathed, confusing her further. "But then you'd be my employee, and I don't want you to be."

"Why not?" Her breath caught. He'd accept? But he still didn't want her?

Slowly he stepped forward. He traced a tender finger along her jaw line. Stopping under her chin, gently lifted her face up to him.

"Because if you're my employee." He whispered huskily, "then I can't do this."

She thought she was going to faint as his lips met hers. Her arms were around him, pulling him into her. She arched her back against him as her tongue danced with his.

His hands were running wild through her loose hair, and her towel dropped to the floor.

She gasped. She had totally forgotten she was naked. He pulled away, and held her at arm's length to get a good look at her. He could not hide his approval.

"Well, I'll be honest," he grinned. "I didn't think it would be quite *that* easy to get you out of your clothes."

"I am so embarrassed right now," she murmured, holding his gaze. She didn't even want to attempt to cover herself up.

"You have nothing to be embarrassed about," he told her huskily, pulling her lips back to meet his.

She pushed him through to the living room, out of the view of the kitchen window, where anyone on the yard could see into her tiny cottage. He pressed her against the wall as his tongue explored her. His day-old stubble scratched against her cheek. He held her by the shoulders, his thumbs skimming her collar bone. He kissed her so tenderly; she crumpled under his every touch. She ran her palm down his chest, feeling the hard muscles through the fabric of his shirt that she longed to rip over his head.

He pulled away breathlessly, wanting another look at her.

"Do you know how long I've been waiting for you to do that?" she whispered.

He licked his already moist lips. "Considering your initial impression of me was not great, probably not as long as I have."

She smiled, her eyes never leaving him as her hands felt down his torso, and pulled his shirt from his jeans. She slipped a hand underneath, skimmed across the ridges of his toned stomach. He had a sharp intake of breath as her cold hands surprised him.

"You need warming up," he murmured.

"Oh yes, do you have something in mind?" she teased.

"Well yes, there is something..." he breathed.

She needed to see this body that every female on the eventing circuit fantasised about; to see whether it really was as good as they all imagined. She slowly unfastened the buttons, and he slipped it off over his broad, strong shoulders.

"Don't tell me you get a body like that just from riding horses?" she gasped, exploring every inch of his sculpted torso with teasing fingertips. It was better than she could ever have imagined.

He closed his eyes, unable to hide his smile. His head tilted back as she brushed her hand over his erection straining at his jeans. Slowly she unclasped his belt buckle.

Cecil growled, threateningly, but Elsa ignored him. She'd been waiting so long for this moment that nothing was going to stop her now. If she turned down the opportunity to get to know this body, she'd never forgive herself.

Frederick hesitated. "Erm, Elsa?" he asked politely, stilling her hands.

He pulled away, and she glared at him, waiting.

He looked sheepish. "Please can you send the dog away? He's putting me off."

She glanced down at her side, where Cecil sat watching them intently, hackles still raised and teeth bared, and smiled. "He's just looking out for me."

"Which I am extremely grateful for, as everyone should have a loyal dog, however..."

"To your bed, Cecil," Elsa told him gently.

He whined and didn't move. "Now," she said, a little more sternly, and he whined even louder and pattered reluctantly through to the kitchen. She turned to Frederick.

"Thank you," he smiled. "Now, where were we?"

She reached up to meet his lips and he responded. She arched her body against his as their tongues danced together. Her body came alive as he trailed fingers sensitively down her back, swept them over her bare behind and underneath her thighs. He lifted her from the ground, her slender legs wrapping eagerly around his waist. He pushed her back against the wall as he kissed her hungrily.

Her shoulders forcefully dislodged the photo frame behind her. Frederick noticed it and stopped. "You have a photo of my horse on your wall," he grinned. "How sweet."

"Hey!" she prodded him in the chest. "He was my horse first, and it's still a touchy subject, so don't go ruining the moment!"

"Why don't we go upstairs?" he murmured, trailing soft kisses down her neck.

She groaned and bit her lower lip. The anticipation was killing her. But a sudden thought gripped her, and she wondered when she had last tidied her bedroom. She hoped there wasn't masses of bras and socks strewn everywhere, clumps of hay and shavings here and there.

Her stomach rumbled, uninvitedly.

"Have you not eaten yet?" Frederick asked her, concerned.

She shook her head. "I've only just got in from the yard and jumped straight in the shower. I'm not sure if you noticed, but I haven't even had a chance to get dressed yet."

"Oh, I barely noticed," he licked his lips. "But I also didn't think. I should have brought something with me. Let's order a takeaway."

She shook her head, desperate not to let him out of her grasp. "We have something much more important to do first."

She loved the feel of his strong, big hands holding her. He didn't stop kissing her as he backed her across the living room to the stairs. Her hands ran wildly through his blond locks of hair, up and down his back, feeling the ridge of muscle either side of his spine.

She felt his erection straining against her, desperate to be unleashed from his jeans. She was so wet for him already; her sex tingled just at the thought of all the glorious things she wanted him to do to her. She pushed herself against him and let out a low moan.

He stopped halfway up the stairs, crushing her against the wall as he rebalanced himself.

"You drive me crazy, Elsa," he told her, his voice husky. His soft blue eyes never left her.

She smiled. She'd never imagined someone as plain as her could ever have such an effect on someone like him.

Her bedroom door was open, and he carried her in, lowering her down onto her bed. She breathed a sigh of relief that she had attempted at least to make her bed before she fled this morning, and there was minimal underwear strewn across the otherwise tidy bedroom floor. She hadn't vacuumed for a while, but no one is perfect.

She hooked her thumbs inside the waistband of his jeans and slid them down. His erection sprung just inches from her face. She pulled him towards her and he slumped down on the bed. She wrapped her slender fingers around his thick shaft, marvelling at the sheer length of it, and moved in slow strokes. He let out a gasp and sunk back into the excessive mound of pillows, as she felt him grow to full hardness in her palm.

He ran his hand through his curls and groaned. She licked her lips and smiled. *Frederick Twemlow was in her bed, totally naked and looking glorious.*

She swirled her tongue around the tip of his hard cock. He brushed her loose hair from her face and tucked it behind her ear, traced his fingers down her cheek and lingered under her chin, tilting it slightly so that she looked up at him. She slid her eager tongue all the way down his shaft and felt him twitch in her mouth.

"Oh God, Elsa!" he murmured.

He had to stop her, or this was going to be over within seconds. And he'd been waiting too long for it to be over in seconds. He pushed her gently back on the bed and hovered above her. He brushed her hair behind her ears with both hands, brushing over her small, silver earrings with admiration. He took hold of her face firmly in both palms.

"Look what you do to me," he whispered, confused blue eyes searching hers. "And you make my riding go to pot."

"Gee, thanks. Is that meant to be a compliment?" she laughed nervously.

"I could compliment you all night," he told her seriously. "But I don't think you'd listen. I don't like distractions, Elsa, so normally I don't have them. But *you*...what are you doing to me?"

"There is so much I'd like you to do to me." She murmured, anxiously biting her bottom lip.

"Is there now?" He brushed his thumb across her lip, and she released it from her teeth.

He traced sensuous kisses down her neck, across her breasts. He pinched her hardened nipple and she jumped with pleasure at the tremors it sent through her body. He took it in his mouth, sucking and flicking and teasing her with his tongue.

She arched her back against him. Her whole body felt like it was on fire, so alive to his touch.

While his fingers caressed her nipples, he traced kisses across her firm, flat stomach. She waited in anticipation as he neared her small mound of pubic hair, and she pushed herself up to meet him as he gently parted her legs and slid a finger inside her.

She writhed beneath him as he quickened his assault, she felt him stretching her. It had been *so* long that she'd forgotten how good it felt. But she couldn't remember anything being *this* good. She clawed at the duvet, wanting to touch him, to run her hands crazily through his hair and across that muscular, sculpted body, but he was just out of reach. She helplessly tried to sit up; clasped his biceps and tried to pull him closer. He smiled and gently took hold of her wrists. She suddenly felt so empty where his fingers had been.

"Please, Frederick!" she panted.

"I can't wait any longer," he smiled, and fumbled around on the floor for his jeans. He took out a large unopened packet of condoms from his pocket, and ripped the plastic off with his teeth.

She eyed the packet with amusement. "Planning on getting *very* lucky tonight, were you?" she asked with raised eyebrows.

"I stopped off at the service station on the way here; they only had family packs. It's good to be prepared, Elsa," he told her huskily, ripping it from the packet and expertly sliding it down his waiting shaft. "Because I know how angry I'd be with myself if we'd got to this moment right here, and we had to stop!" He left out the bit of how he'd driven like an absolute maniac in order to reach her.

Elsa sighed. She was so ready for him that it didn't bare thinking about. Gently he pushed her back on the bed, held her tiny wrists above her head with one hand. Her loose, damp hair fell around her face, and he brushed it aside.

His cock was poised teasingly against her.

"*Please*," she murmured, trying to push against him, but he held her still as he trailed soft kisses from her lips, down her chest. She stirred as he took her nipple in his teeth; writhed as he flicked his tongue across her belly button. He released her wrists from his gentle grip, but she did not move them.

He twisted her small, neat strip of pubic hair around his long fingers; fingers that had felt so good inside her. She gasped as he teased them along her folds, gently probed into her opening and delighted at how wet she was for him.

She arched her back; so sure he was going to enter her, and whimpered as he retreated and trailed those delightful lips along the inside of her thigh; across her groin. She gasped as his tongue found her folds; lapping at her nub. She felt her ecstasy building, all of her senses gone off the scale as the pressure all became too much. She felt her whole body convulsing; she gave herself to him entirely as his tongue moved deeper, feeling her trembles and slowing as he waited for her orgasm to finish.

"You're so beautiful, Elsa," he told her, kissing her *there*. It felt like a buzz of electricity, making her jump and smile.

But she couldn't reply; she could barely speak.

"Was that one of the things you wanted me to do to you?" he murmured.

"God *yes*," she croaked.

Her body was laced with a thin layer of sweat, and he licked his lips as he kissed it away. But he really could not wait any longer; he'd waited long enough. He nudged her legs slightly further apart, running his hands down her sensuously smooth legs he clasped her ankles. He pushed them forward, bending her knees.

She cried out as he swiftly entered her. Her eyes were large with surprise as he pushed his cock in up to the hilt. He thrust gently, slowly at first, and she eagerly met each one, as gradually he quickened.

She already felt her second orgasm brewing. He felt it too, and waited inside her for her writhing to stop.

"So close," she exhaled, knowing that he had stopped her on purpose and thinking him to be rather cruel.

He withdrew so tantalisingly slowly, brushing his swollen tip along her folds that it made her quiver.

"That feels *so* good," she murmured. "*Please.*"

His hands firmly around her buttocks, he drove into her once more. He slowly withdrew again, but there was no teasing her anymore, just satisfaction as he devoured her. She clasped his hair, the feeling of his hot, sticky body pressed hard against hers sending her further into a crazed frenzy as he slowly thrust in and out of her.

She felt it nearing, and grasped him tight as she erupted, biting his shoulder to muffle her cries.

"That's it, Elsa!" he growled. "That's *it!*" And he pummelled into her ball deep and stilled as he reached his own climax. She felt his cock twitching inside her, which only intensified her own feeling.

Finally their bodies stilled, and he held her. She didn't want him to ever let go. He laid her back down, her eyes closed in pure bliss, plumping the pillows before placing her head onto them. She gasped as he withdrew from her. He had been reluctant to, and was grateful now for buying the family pack of condoms. He could already feel he would be requiring them again soon.

She shivered and he pulled the duvet around them both, planting a tender kiss on her forehead, and stretched out alongside her; their spent bodies entwined.

"That was better than I'd ever possibly imagined," he murmured, gently stroking her chaotic hair. He was so glad he had left his mother's party early. Ava was good company and fought off his family's probing relationship questions with confidence and grace, he could trust her and couldn't imagine being without her, but they'd never be an item. Thank God she didn't like him, Frederick thought with a grateful sigh, and thank God that Elsa appeared to and was adamant she didn't want the job. He really believed this could work between them. He enjoyed her company. She was beautiful, and she made him laugh and lose his mind. And she had just given him the most wonderful sex. He could get used to waking up beside her.

She opened her eyes; he was looking right at her. She didn't know what to say; she was still on cloud nine and no words felt appropriate. Did she agree with him? Did she thank him? He smiled and pulled her into his chest, and together their tired bodies succumbed to sleep.

Chapter Ten

Elsa's stomach rumbled and she rolled over and stretched out, but something stopped her. She smiled, remembering her blissful night and so happy that it hadn't actually just been a dream. She opened her eyes. The room was in darkness but his bright, blue eyes shone as he watched her.

"Hello, sleepy head," he smiled, unable to hide his contentment.

She smiled as she trailed a finger gingerly across his stubble. He wrapped his arms around her and pulled her into him, smothering her in tender kisses. She giggled as his stubble ticked her suddenly over-sensitive skin. His touch sent tingles down to her groin. She felt his cock twitch against her thigh as their naked bodies pressed together.

She was only a little sore from his surprised entrance, but she couldn't wait to do it again. She was already getting wet just from the thought of it...

Her stomach growled again, and he pulled away.

"You've still not eaten," he frowned, annoyed at himself for having forgotten.

"It's OK, I'm not hungry anymore," she told him.

"That's a lie," he murmured. "That's like you telling me that you don't want me," he paused, running a finger between her legs and feeling how wet she was. "When your body clearly tells me that you do."

She gasped as he slid a finger into her. She reached for his cock and stroked it quickly to full hardness. He had already located the condom box with one hand as his fingers continued to slide in and out of her.

He ripped the foil off with his teeth, and she took it from him and slid it onto his erection. He flipped her over easily onto her front, and she didn't object as he hoisted the most beautiful rear he had ever seen up towards him. The sight on her on her knees and elbows at his mercy, her head twisted around so she could get a good look at him, drove him crazy.

His hands gripped her hips as he hungrily drove his cock into her. She cried out and grasped hold of the bed sheet, pushing back to feel as much of him as she could fit inside of her.

"*Yes!*" she begged, as he withdrew and thrust into her harder.

Her messy hair fell across her slender shoulders, swinging as she arched to meet each thrust. He gathered it up and twisted it in his palm, careful not to tug it. He didn't want to hurt her, but he loved her hair.

She groaned as his balls swung against her, sending pleasure surging through her. He powerfully thrust back into her, and felt his climax nearing.

He reached around her waist and brushed his palm against her clit. She panted; the satisfaction of his touch absolutely exhilarating. Her breasts swung with each thrust, and Frederick took them both in his palms, squeezing them hard and flicking her nipples. She gasped and moved her own hand between her legs, rubbing her clit in mesmerising circles until she couldn't take any more.

She panted, her face pushed down into the pillow to muffle her cries as her body exploded around his satisfied cock.

His thrusts intensified and he cried out in unison with her, slowing as he emptied his load. He held her for a moment until they both came back to earth.

She slumped on her arms, her breathing calming. He trailed kisses up her back, the nape of her neck, gently nibbling on her earlobe.

"Now do let me get you something to eat?" he whispered.

She nodded; her mouth so dry she wasn't sure she could talk, let alone eat. She stretched out on her bed, her eyes closed as suddenly she felt very sleepy again, and he tucked the duvet around her.

He searched around on the floor for his boxers, found them tangled with his jeans and pulled them on.

"I'll see what I can find," he promised, with a tender, parting kiss.

"You are coming back, aren't you?" she asked nervously.

"Elsa," he smiled. "Whether I come back or not only really depends on whether your dog eats me."

She watched him leave, rolled over and let out a large sigh of delight. She hadn't felt this good in a long while. Her bed smelled of him, her body smelled of him, and it was absolutely *divine*.

Cecil's sharp, ferocious bark stopped her from drifting off. She bolted upright.

"Er...Elsa?" Frederick called nervously.

"Cecil!" she shouted, her voice raspy. She waited. "Cecil!"

She heard the thud of his paws as he excitedly ascended the stairs, bounded through the door and sprung onto her bed. He immediately curled up and resumed his nap. Elsa pulled him into her chest, hoping her happiness would rub off on him.

"He's not a bad person," she whispered into his shaggy ear.

Cecil yawned, his big, brown eyes telling her that he definitely felt otherwise.

"Are you sure you're not French?" Frederick enquired, returning a moment later with a tray. He checked the coast was clear from snarling teeth before he entered. Cecil regarded him quietly.

Elsa opened her eyes and frowned.

"All you seem to have in this house is cheese, bread and wine!" Frederick laughed.

She smiled. "I hope you brought all three up with you? Sounds like heaven."

He paused as Cecil lifted his head and thought about growling at him.

"I'm not sure about this dog, Elsa," he murmured, eyeing his competitor.

"The dog is make or break," she held his beautiful blue eyes.

"OK," Frederick shrugged quickly. "I'm fine with the dog."

He climbed back into bed and presented her with the tray. A bottle of red wine, and slices of fresh cut bread, a various assortment of sliced cheeses, and a dollop of what she assumed was the chutney her mother insisted on sending her. She licked her lips, suddenly hungry. Frederick watched with raised eyebrows as she devoured the selection.

"What?" she asked innocently between mouthfuls. "This is pretty much what I live on."

The alarm clock just wouldn't be quiet, and Elsa really wished it would. The shrill ring went right through her, rousing her from her deep sleep. She lashed out to quieten it, and in her haste, she smacked the blond-haired beauty laying beside her, right across the face. Her guilt was quickly replaced with glee that he was still here, that he hadn't woken before her and slipped out, never to be seen again.

"I swear I've only been asleep five minutes." She yawned, reluctant to get up.

"Don't worry about me," he smiled, already awake. "I don't mind being clouted if it means I get to wake up next to you every morning."

She blinked herself awake, squinting into the light seeping in around the curtains. He ran a finger tenderly across her cheek, his blue eyes imploring her.

"Why did you text me?" Elsa asked eventually. "That time, a few days after I'd taken Nobby to you."

"Because I wanted to see you again," he murmured, tracing tender fingers along her soft skin. "Desperately so. And then, when I watched you arrive at the yard, I knew how absurd it would look if I dashed out to greet you, so I told Ava I was going out. But I so desperately wanted to, believe me."

"I was so angry at you."

"Yes, I got that impression. I'm sorry that I took your horse, but I'm also not sorry, because it meant I got to meet you."

"I want to hate you for taking him," she murmured, suddenly feeling emotional.

"Please don't hate me, Elsa," he whispered, trailing kisses along her collar bone.

"But why me? Why plain, boring little me?" she asked nervously. "You could have your pick of, well...*anyone*. I'm just a groom."

"You're not plain or boring," he looked offended on her behalf. "Neither are you *just a groom*. You're funny, strong, independent and *immensely* beautiful. And you've never tried to impress me, Elsa. I like that. I've never had to work so hard for someone in all my life as I have for you. I was impressed we didn't touch each other before – but it made me more determined. I knew you'd be worth the wait." He wrapped his arms around her and pulled her into his chest. She willed away threatening tears, desperately hoping he wouldn't see how moist her eyes had become.

What is wrong with me? She inwardly cursed herself. It wasn't like her to cry and get all emotional. But she had had the best night of her life, and she could happily stay in his arms forever. She had no urgency to get up, but her horses needed her, just as Frederick's probably needed him.

With a parting kiss on her forehead, Frederick released her and climbed from the bed. He wanted to stay there forever, but his horses needed him and if he held her much longer, parts of his body would start to respond, and then he wasn't sure if he'd ever leave.

"Mind if I take a shower?" he asked her, and she rolled over to see one last glimpse of him standing before her in just his boxers, suddenly looking very shy.

"Of course," she smiled. "The bathroom's the door opposite; no chance of getting lost in this little house. There's clean towels on the rack."

He nodded and left. She smiled and snuggled up into the duvet, pulling it to her and smelling the strong scent of him and never wanting to wash her bed sheets again. She listened to the sound of running water and whistled for Cecil, who at some point during the night had disappeared back downstairs to resume chief guard dog duties. He came bounding up the stairs and stopped at the door, wondering what was keeping her from delivering his breakfast. His ears followed the sound of running water in confusion, and he barked. She patted the bed and he ran towards her and bounded up onto it.

But his hackles went up and he growled as the shower stopped and Frederick stepped from the bathroom, looking fresh and divine with just a towel around his waist. Elsa restrained her hound, with a grin on her face.

"What are you grinning at?" Frederick murmured, nearing her but keeping his distance from ferocious Cecil.

"You," she smiled.

He reached down and cupped her face in his palms, kissing her softly.

"I'm sorry I have to go," he murmured.

"Me too," she told him. "Can I get you anything to eat first?"

He shook his head. "I have to get back, Ava will have my first horse ready and be calling me all the names under the sun. Normally I'm very punctual," he shook his head, searching her eyes. "*Normally*. What are you doing to me, Elsa?" He met her lips and she didn't want him to go. Reluctantly he pulled away, searching for his clothes crumpled on the floor and pulling them on, and Elsa gave a silent, sad goodbye to his sculpted body.

"Your shirt is downstairs," she told him, smiling at the memories.

He smiled too. He kissed her again, reluctant to leave her. "I'll let myself out. I'll call you, OK?"

She nodded, and watched him leave. *God, I'm scared*, she told herself. Relationships didn't last where your horses were your number one priority and you were so often on the road. They would get pulled in different directions. She should know; she'd tried. She was only twenty-six, yet had already resigned herself to the fact that while her friends had normal jobs and were settling down, her life she had chosen for herself would probably always consist mainly of horses and sleeping irregular hours in lorries. But maybe she and Frederick were more alike than she wanted to think. Elsa was a hard worker and a perfectionist, too. *But I'm scared of letting someone into my life who diverts my attention away from my work,* her mind spun. Someone who didn't understand that she both needed and wanted to be up at the crack of dawn, that her aspirations were helping Sophia get to where she deserved to be on the eventing circuit, and then who knows where that would take them both. But surely Frederick was the best one to understand that?

But Elsa loved her independence; she loved it being just her and Cecil, not having to consider the needs of anyone else. Her life was busy enough as it was.

She pulled the duvet around her, taking one long, last smell of him before she herself jumped in the shower. Sophia would be out on the yard soon, looking for her first horse. She needed to shove any further thoughts of Frederick Twemlow, firmly to one side.

Elsa fed the horses with a definite spring in her step; not even shouting at Drop Kick as he banged impatiently against his stable door. She even found herself humming as she stuffed haylage into nets.

It had been forty minutes since Frederick had left, and she already missed him. She let herself into Connor's box and he gave her a very bemused look as she set about brushing him with a new sense of determination and a little smile that she was unable to conceal. She felt radiant. Also a little sore, but mainly *radiant.*

Connor shoved his nose obligingly into his bridle and Elsa smoothed down his saddlecloth. There was no sign of Sophia yet, so she put on her hat and tightened the geldings girth, and climbed aboard to get him worked in. If Elsa was tired, she did not show it, and when Connor tried to take off with her down the long side of the manège, she quickly pulled him up and told him that she meant business. The gelding could tell she was not joking, either, and duly obliged. He was feeling fabulous by the time Sophia strolled across the yard.

"Morning!" Elsa called cheerfully, easing the gelding to a halt readying to hand over the reins.

"What the bloody hell was Freddy Twemlow's Range Rover doing parked outside your cottage all night?" Sophia demanded, unable to keep the grin from her face.

Elsa jumped to the floor and spun around to meet her, her eyes wide with shock. "Oh, you noticed?" she asked feebly.

"Of course I noticed!" she replied, amused. "A beast of a car with a personalised plate! It doesn't exactly blend in, Elsa."

Elsa turned back around as if adjusting the length of Connor's stirrups required her undivided attention. She inwardly cursed herself for thinking no one would see, but she wasn't ready for this. She wasn't ready to share her secret, she wanted to let it all sink in first.

"Well, come on then!" Sophia demanded excitedly. "*Spill!*"

Elsa shrugged. She turned back around, but couldn't meet her eye. Neither could she keep the coy smile from her face.

"And don't try and fob me off with the old *he stayed all night but nothing happened bullshit...*"

"It wouldn't be the first time," Elsa finally met her eye, and Sophia frowned. "That he stayed all night and nothing happened," Elsa explained to her confused look.

"Oh my God! You're a dark horse! *When?*" Sophia asked excitedly. "How long has this been going on?"

"Nothing is going on," Elsa insisted, with a shrug. "But at

Picton, after the cross country... Well, he came over to the lorry to keep me company. I was horrible to him, trying to get him to leave. Well, half-heartedly. I so badly wanted to hate him for taking Nobby. But I couldn't hate him; he was so nice, and he helped me clean tack."

"Frederick Twemlow *cleaned* my tack?" Sophia exclaimed in disbelief.

"Yea," Elsa replied with a shrug.

"Wow! But he stayed?" Sophia hurried her excitedly.

Elsa slowly nodded.

"Like, in the same bed?" Sophia was practically jumping from foot to foot.

She nodded again.

"And *nothing* happened?" Sophia gawped, incredulous.

"Nothing," Elsa murmured, Connor nudging her in the back in case she had forgotten him.

"How the hell did you spend all night laying alongside that body and *not* touch it? Is it as good in the flesh as we all imagine it to be? Well, all of us except you, as you'd have us all believe."

"It really is," Elsa sighed. "And it was hard." She admitted.

"I bet it was!" Sophia exclaimed, and they both giggled like school girls.

"So, last night?" Sophia went on, eventually calming herself. "What happened?"

Connor impatiently pawed at the ground, and Elsa wished he'd make a bit more of a fuss so that she could be relieved of any more questions.

"Well, we, you know... do I really have to spell it out?" Elsa looked all around her except at Sophia.

"Oh, my God! You *didn't*?" Sophia's eyes were wide.

Elsa nodded, suddenly exceptionally embarrassed.

Sophia gave her a high five, her smile wide. "You go, girl!" she exclaimed.

"You're not annoyed?" Elsa asked gently.

"Annoyed?" she was perplexed. "Why the hell would I be annoyed?"

"He took your best horse. I feel like such a traitor."

"That's just business," Sophia shrugged. "And who cares about business when you're getting laid by the most *good looking*, eligible bachelor on the circuit? Annoyed, I am not. But I am rather jealous, along with every other girl out there!"

"No one needs be jealous," Elsa said quietly. "Because no one knows. Plus, it was just one night; I might never see him again."

"Oh! Don't go all coy on me," Sophia laughed. "I'd be shouting it from the rooftops if he'd looked twice at me! When *are* you seeing him again?"

Elsa shrugged.

"Do you want to see him again?" Sophia probed.

She slowly nodded.

"How long have you been chasing him?"

"I haven't..."

"What? This is all him?" Sophia bounced with excitement. She had *so* many questions.

Elsa nodded.

"Wow! That's unheard of! He must really like you!"

"Don't..." she said shyly, wanting her to stop.

"No way! Don't be all shy and modest! This is *exciting*!"

Connor nipped her arm. "Ok! Relax, I'm coming!" Sophia told him, and Elsa legged her into the saddle.

"So, has he called you yet?" Sophia asked, circling Connor around her.

"No," Elsa laughed, trying to back away. "He's barely been gone five minutes!"

"True," Sophia shrugged, and suddenly her face lit up again. "Don't his parents have a title? Does that mean he'll inherit it? Like couldn't you marry him and became a *Lady*?" Sophia could not stop the giggles that followed. "A *Lady*!" She squealed. "Can you imagine – *Lady Elsa?*"

"Stop!" Elsa pleaded. "It's all too much. I still can't quite believe it myself, but I just want to see where it goes. He might not even want to see me again."

"Oh, he will, *Lady Elsa!*" Sophia winked, but suddenly the smile dropped from her face and she reined Connor to face her. "Shit! Elsa, the other day, when I said about the job...does this mean you're going to go and work for him?"

"What? No!" Elsa exclaimed. "Absolutely no way, Sophia."

"I know he'd have you in a shot and he'd probably pay you double what you get at mine." Sophia told her sullenly.

"Are you trying to get rid of me?" Elsa laughed.

"God no! But he's...*you know.*"

"No way, Sophia," Elsa insisted. "There is *no* way I'd work for him, and I'm very happy here."

"I'm so relieved." She smiled, nudging Connor on.

Elsa smiled and turned away, glad that this conversation appeared it would go no further, and she could get back to her stable duties.

Beep beep. Her mobile chirped in her pocket, stopping her in her tracks. She nervously bit her lip, hoping Sophia hadn't heard. But Sophia had already stopped, and was glaring at her.

"Is that *him*?" she demanded excitedly.

Connor irritably snatched at the bit; he had work to be getting on with was far more important than this gossip, but Sophia made him wait.

Elsa pulled her mobile from the pocket and stared at the screen.

Thanks for last night, I had a really good time. See you soon for round two ;-) Fred x

She took a deep breath and silently read it again. Sophia was waiting. She impatiently tapped Elsa on the shoulder with her whip, craning to see the screen.

"*Well?*" she demanded. "Is it him? What did he say?"

"It's just a friend," Elsa clasped her phone to her chest and spun around in a gleeful circle, facing Sophia with a massive grin. "Honest!" And she broke into a gentle jog to the gate.

"Oh, you *devil*!" Sophia chased her across the manège. "Show me that message *now,* you liar!"

"No time!" Elsa laughed, springing over the fence with more energy than a racehorse, and crossing the yard. "I've got work to be getting on with it!" She shouted over her shoulder, poking out her tongue.

"I will get all the nitty, gritty details out of you later, *Lady*!" Sophia bellowed after her, waving her stick, and she pushed Connor into a trot with a shake of her head.

Elsa was still on cloud nine, and she desperately wanted to see him again. But with the combination of both of them having heavy workloads, she knew there wouldn't be much risk of her throwing herself at him easily. Sophia had several one day events lined up for the young horses, to ease both them and her injured limbs back into competition. Mostly they were local, but it was still a long day for Elsa nonetheless when she still had a yard full of horses to tend to before and after attending any events. And since Frederick's helpful pointers with Bear, Elsa was determined to keep the fiery mare ticking over and get her back out to her own competition soon.

She managed to avoid Sophia's inquisitions, and retired to her cottage to call her mother before taking an afternoon nap. She gave herself a long look in the bathroom mirror and smiled. She felt so *happy*. After the heartache of losing Nobby, things had just started to go right recently. She wasn't sure if she could attribute all her heartache and all her happiness to the one, same person though. She knew she had a lot to be happy about, as Cecil proved as he pattered into the bathroom and watched her with amusement as she danced and sang in the steaming shower.

Her bed felt so big and empty since Frederick had departed, even though Cecil tried his best to take up most of it. She turned her phone over in her hand, willing him to call her and wondering if she should text. But what if he didn't want to see her again? What if he really had got all that he had wanted, and she really was just a notch on Frederick Twemlow's bedpost. She sighed, and Cecil gave her a knowing look.

"I know," she told the shaggy mutt. "You wouldn't be surprised, you never liked him anyway."

She closed her eyes, but opened them quickly with a start as her mobile beeped.

Missing you. Fred x, the display read.

She whooped with joy and Cecil leapt up, startled, and considered abandoning ship. She put her arm around him and hugged him tightly.

"He misses me, Cec," she told him, rubbing his belly. He yawned and lay back down. Her heart warmed, she pulled the duvet over her head to block out the light, and dialled her old house number. She would have a brief check in with her mother, and then she really needed to catch some sleep.

"I'm going to try a horse this afternoon," Sophia told her the following morning. "If it goes well you can pick it up tomorrow – they've agreed to a month's trial."

Elsa smiled, liking the positive tone of her voice. There was still no sign of Christine Forrester's promised youngsters, and while it narked Elsa a little, the only consolation was not having that hideous woman swooping onto the yard at any minute.

Just please don't let it be grey! Elsa prayed. They had enough greys already – it was the bane of her life trying to scrub yellow stable stains off of their many greys.

She set off across the yard and grabbed a broom. The morning's mucking out had left various trails of straw that Elsa set about sweeping. She jumped as her mobile phone started ringing in her pocket, and she excitedly reached for it.

Mum, the display read, and Elsa immediately felt guilty as her heart sank. She was conscious of Sophia's eye following her as she hit the answer button, and went around the corner of the barn out of earshot.

"Was that him?" Sophia demanded excitedly at her groom's return.

"No," Elsa rolled her eyes at her persistence, and continued with her sweeping. "It was just my mother letting me know some dates that I can go and visit her this month." She only lived a couple of hours away, yet Elsa still struggled to find the time to visit.

"Oh." Sophia replied. "You were hoping it was him though, weren't you?"

"Maybe," Elsa sighed, not even bothering to shield her disappointment.

"Have you seen him since?"

She shook her head.

"It was only *yesterday* that I last saw him, Sophia!" Elsa scolded. "Honestly, you're keener than I am!"

"So what!" Sophia laughed. "You can't let ones like that get away!"

"He has text me, though." Elsa added quickly.

"*Saying?*"

"Sophia!" Elsa laughed. "I am never going to get this yard swept if you don't leave me alone!"

"Screw the yard!" Sophia scowled. "Tell me *now*. What did it say?"

"Just little things," she shrugged, feeling her stomach flutter. "Like *missing you* and *can't wait to see you again*."

"These are *big* things!" Sophia swooned. "He wants to see you again! Do you want to see him again?"

"Of course," she replied coyly. "Who wouldn't?"

"Do you think about him all day and every day?" Sophia smiled.

Slowly Elsa nodded, feeling her cheeks redden. "Mostly."

"You've got it bad, haven't you?"

She nodded without hesitation. "Horribly. It's amazing how one, little, small text can brighten up someone's day, isn't it? I've always thought I didn't need a guy to do that for me. Normally just my mum checking on me is enough to put a spring in my step, or Cecil's cute little face following me around the yard, but this..." she broke off, feeling her stomach somersault.

"But?" Sophia probed.

"Well, this is just *different*. Good different, and I really like it."

Sophia squealed with delight and threw her arms around her.

"I'm *so* happy!" she announced. "I *so* hope this works out for you!"

Elsa embraced her, laughing. "So do I," she shrugged. "Now let me get on with my work," she told her, sternly. "And haven't you got a horse to go and see?"

Chapter Eleven

As it happened, Sophia loved the little mare, who apparently behaved like a Drama Queen and was aptly named Candy, and Elsa was to pick her up the next day. She was going for a good price, from a good home where she had been slowly and correctly produced, and Sophia saw potential in her.

"I wasn't looking for anything new, but someone mentioned her," Sophia told her, as she made them a cup of tea in the tack room. "And well, with Drop Kick off... I can't afford another of his calibre, can I? And no one seems to be bringing any our way. I'm going to have to make myself another one."

"Never thought I'd hear myself say this, but I'd be quite grateful to see Christine Forrester pull into the yard right now." Elsa replied.

"She must have got a better offer," Sophia added through gritted teeth. She squeezed the teabag out and tossed it in the bin in anger. "Anyway," she forced a smile. "One more to take to the baby classes won't do any harm, will it? And at least if I own it, no one can take it away from me."

"Things will pick up," Elsa smiled. "The horses we have got are going really well – baby classes or not – and we should be thankful."

"I know," Sophia sighed. "You're right, as always."

There was the sound of crunching gravel, and the girls peered out as the familiar car of one of their few remaining owners pulled to a halt. Gilly leapt out, riding clothes on and hat in hand.

"Beautiful day for a ride, isn't it?" Gilly beamed.

"Lovely!" The girls replied in unison.

"How is my best, most beautiful boy?" she crowed,

bypassing them and dashing straight to Connor's stable.

"He's doing great," Sophia replied with a smile.

"He is looking absolutely *gorgeous*," Gilly beamed, looking over the stable door of her best boy, as he nuzzled her pockets for treats. "I'm sorry I couldn't make it last weekend," she rolled her eyes, referring to Connor's run at Picton. "But the kids wanted to go to the zoo... and... well, you know how it is."

Sophia nodded sympathetically. She had debriefed Gilly over the phone as soon as they'd returned home, but she knew how much it meant to Gilly to be able to see him perform in the flesh.

"Want me to get him ready?" Elsa asked, knowing that Gilly would refuse.

"Don't be silly," Gilly smiled. "You know I love it. And don't you dare touch his stable; I'll muck him out when I get back!"

Elsa didn't argue, and prepared Merlin for Sophia.

"I hear that you and Timber Bear had a good run at Nelson?" Gilly called from the tack room.

"Yes, she was brilliant!" Elsa told her, her smile wide whenever she talked about her little mare. "I didn't show her up for once, either."

"I'm sure you were fab!" Gilly laughed, stepping back out onto the yard weighed down with Connor's tack. "You shouldn't put yourself down so much!"

If Elsa wished any owner could bring them more horses, then it would be Gilly. Gilly was one of their most favoured owners, and both girls adored her. She had bought Connor as a riding horse for herself, but was the first to admit his talents quickly outgrew hers, and as her time was increasingly taken over by her growing family, she had handed the reins over to Sophia a year ago, and never looked back. She absolutely loved coming to watch him at events, and hacking him out at home whenever time allowed, and Elsa was always grateful for having one less to ride. But Gilly would not allow herself to school her cherished mount, she left that to the professionals.

Elsa legged them both up onto their horses, checked their girths and sent them on their way. She would do Merlin's stable while they were out, replenish all the haynets, and then she would be done for the afternoon. She needed to go into town and do her weekly shop; she had been ignoring her empty fridge for three days now, but Cecil had munched through his last tin of dog food this morning, and there was no way he would let her back in to the cottage empty handed.

She was collecting empty haynets as her mobile began to ring, and she was grateful that Sophia was well out of earshot and she could avoid her invasive questions. She snatched it from her pocket and her heart skipped a beat at the caller display. *Frederick.*

"Hey," his voice was smooth. He sounded almost hesitant – did she detect a certain shyness? "Missed me?" he laughed nervously.

She smiled. She'd been missing him since the minute he'd departed her bed. "Of course," she replied.

"I was wondering if your little mare had recovered from her run at Nelson at the weekend and you wanted to bring her over?"

She wondered briefly if she'd heard him right. She'd feared his offer had not been serious, and she hadn't wanted to get her hopes up, as she had never heard that Frederick was ever subject to such generous offers.

"It's OK if you don't want to," he noticed her hesitation. "I just thought..."

"Of course I want to," she quickly cut him off, before he could backtrack. "It's so nice of you to offer."

"How about tomorrow?"

She closed her eyes in disappointment. "I can't tomorrow, I have to go and pick up a new horse."

"Hmm, next week then?" he suggested.

She tried to keep her disappointment from her voice. She had been so excited about the impending new arrival, but now it seemed it was going to keep her from seeing him for even longer.

"Next week," she forced a smile.

"It's a date," he laughed.

"Any excuse to see my horse, eh?" she teased. "Are you sure you're not after her, too?"

"She's a lovely horse, Elsa, but I'm much more interested in her rider." His voice was husky, and she felt her heart leap with his words.

The next morning Elsa swung the lorry through the tight gates of a little local livery yard, and was greeted by a tearful teenager clinging to the lead rope of a gorgeous dun mare who looked more like an overgrown pony.

"I'm going to Uni and I can't take her with me," she explained to Elsa as they lowered the lorry ramp. "She's wasted with me anyway, she has so much potential, even if she doesn't look like it."

"Well, Sophia must have seen something in her," Elsa smiled, very much liking the look of the little mare.

"I am *so* glad Sophia liked her; I couldn't imagine a better owner for her. I really hope she behaves herself at yours," she hesitated, rubbing the mare's ears affectionately. "She can actually be really naughty," the girl warned. "She *is* a handful at home, she needs a varied life, but once you get her out to a competition she absolutely knows her job."

"It'll be nothing I'm not used to," Elsa reassured her. "Don't worry, she'll have the best possible care at ours."

The teenager nodded, wiping away stray tears, and Elsa was reminded of herself when she had to take Nobby to Frederick Twemlow's. *Nobby*, dear little Nobby. And *Frederick Twemlow*, arrogant, rude, top-ride stealing arsehole – who had turned out to be anything but that. Her heart fluttered just at the thought of him.

The teenager was chucking armfuls of rugs and tack into the lorry. "I told Sophia you might as well have them," she shrugged at Elsa's confused look. "I bought them all for her, and I've no used for them now."

"Has Sophia told you that you can come and visit?" Elsa asked.

The teenager nodded. "She said any time."

"Well do, won't you?" Elsa implored. "Candy would love to see you, I'm sure, and I could always do with a friend to hack out with."

"Thank you," she smiled gratefully. "I would really like that."

She handed Elsa the mare's lead rope, who duly dug her heels in as Elsa pointed her to the ramp.

"Some days she walks straight in," the teenager shrugged. "Some days not at all."

Elsa turned her and walked her back to the ramp. The mare stopped and Elsa tried her again.

"She'll get bored before I do," Elsa told the teenager, and proceeded to keep the mare walking until she was happy to board. Ten minutes later, and her nose was tucked gratefully into her waiting haynet, the partition closed on her and the ramp up, and Elsa was swinging the lorry back out of the narrow gate, aware that the sobbing teenager was watching her all the way down the drive.

It was a straightforward journey home, and Elsa could hardly tell she had Candy in the back as the mare was so quiet. She unloaded her and put her straight out into one of the sand paddocks; small turnout areas where the horses could stretch their legs but not build up any speed nor fill their bellies with rich grass.

She tried to sniff noses with Merlin over the fence, gave a squeal and a kick when she could not reach, and went off at a beautiful extended trot with her tail held high and flowing out behind her.

"She certainly will turn heads," Elsa smiled pleasingly, watching her. Anything that got Sophia noticed but couldn't be taken away from her, was very welcome.

She gave a wave as Derek's car pulled into the yard, and went off to saddle Connor, to find Sophia had already done it.

"Blossom could do with going out too, if you fancy it?" Sophia asked.

Sophia nodded and gladly took Blossom's tack from the rack instead. Blossom was a young coloured cob who had suffered some confidence issues with her novice owners, and so had been sent to Sophia for schooling. Elsa quite liked her, and it was not a chore hacking her out. The gentle little mare just needed constant reassurance to put one hoof in front of the other, but she'd improved so much in the week that that she'd been here. Elsa wondered though if she'd always be too much for her current owners and if they'd ask if she could stay on as a sales livery.

Sophia joined her afterwards, and they took Merlin and Ruby for some fast work up the gallops, in preparation for their next event the following week. Merlin was a little over-excited, and as usual Sophia had a job on her hands to contain him, but Ruby duly worked nicely by his side, ignoring her stable mate's silly antics.

Elsa felt absolutely drained by the time she returned home and washed the horses off. She brought Candy in and settled her into her new stable. She summoned up the energy to whizz Bear around on the lunge for twenty minutes, then checked all the horses had hay and water before retiring to her little cottage.

She kicked off her boots and went straight to the sofa, switched the television on and made way for Cecil to scramble onto her lap, completely blocking her view.

Beep beep. Her phone chirped, and she rearranged Cecil to

retrieve it from her pocket.

Fancy dinner? Feels like forever since I last saw you. Fred x

Her smile lit up her face. She so desperately wanted to see him, but she also desperately didn't want to move from this sofa now she was so comfy. Dinner and seeing Frederick required effort; she would need to shower and at least brush her hair. And find something nice to wear if he was going to take her somewhere posh again. She suddenly possessed a new burst of energy.

Her stomach growled helplessly and Cecil yawned. He jumped to the floor and pattered to his empty bowl, and looked at her longingly.

"Guess if I have to get up to feed you, I may as well drag myself to see Fred?" she smiled gleefully, a definite new spring to her step. "Oh, what a *chore!*"

She jumped straight in the shower, ran the razor over her legs and soaped her hair. She would try and style it slightly better than the *dragged-through-a-hedge* look she pulled off on the yard. But she was no miracle worker, and she towel-dried it and scrunched mousse into it to give some bouncy curls.

She found a pretty floral dress to wear, not stunning but comfortable and appropriate for dinner. She wanted to look as nice as possible without drawing too much attention to herself – Fred did that enough for the pair of them. Everywhere she had been with him, all eyes had been on him, and she had been able to happily just blend into the background.

She declined the offer of a lift, he would have to come out of his way to get her first, and she didn't want to be indebted to him. While his car was impressive and she didn't mind being chauffeured, she enjoyed the time to herself she got from sitting in her little, junk-filled Fiat, tapping her palms against the steering wheel as she belted out some old-school tunes.

Town was quiet, and she easily found a parking space. She assumed Tuesday night was a less popular evening for people to go to dinner. She checked her hair in the tiny rear mirror before stepping outside. She carried her jacket, it being a lovely summer's evening but no doubt she would be chilly later. She grabbed her bag from the backseat, and chucked her mobile and car keys in with the endless old receipts.

Frederick was waiting for her by the fountain in the centre of town, as promised. She was grateful; she hated walking into restaurants alone and standing there like a lemon looking around for the recognisable face among the diners.

He was sitting on the wall to the fountain as she rounded the corner, and she paused to take in the sight of him. He sat so casual, hands in pockets as he tapped his heel against the stone wall, staring at the floor as though deep in thought. He wore navy jeans, brown brogues and a checked shirt. She smiled. He could be wearing a boiler suit and still look perfect.

He looked around and caught her eye, and his face immediately lit up in a smile.

"Hey!" he stood up and came to her, and she took a deep breath of his glorious, familiar aftershave as he tenderly kissed her cheek. "You look great!"

She felt her cheeks reddening already. "This? It's just an old dress I had," she shrugged. "Nothing special."

"You are too modest," he told her, slipping his arm around her waist as he guided her to the High Street. "I chose against Italian food this time, as it didn't seem to go down too well last time."

"It wasn't the food; I've said I'm sorry!" she laughed.

"Was it the company?" he pulled her closer, so that her head nestled into his chest, and stopped.

She looked up at him, her eyes searching his. "The company was...*daunting*," she admitted.

"I hope you're over that now?" he asked quietly, his soft blue eyes never leaving her.

Slowly she nodded.

"And your appetite has returned?" he teased.

"Oh, yes," she smiled, not lying. "I could literally eat a horse!"

"Good!" he laughed, brushing his thumb across her lip. She *so* wanted him to kiss her, to feel his lips on hers again, but he seemed hesitant.

"So, what have you gone for this time?" she enquired.

"French!" he grinned. "They do the best wines, bread and cheese. But of course, they have many other dishes if you fancy a change from that."

She giggled at his thoughtfulness.

"Come on," he took her hand and they were walking again. "It's just this one over here."

The restaurant was a pricey one, and for this reason alone Elsa would never have chosen it to eat out at with friends. She would still offer to pay her share of the bill though, even though she was sure he would decline her offer, she hated to feel indebted to anyone. Their table was nestled cosily in the corner by the window, with a decorative tea light and small vase of flowers.

"Wine?" Frederick asked, as their waiter loitered.

"Not for me, thanks. I have to drive."

"You should have let me pick you up," he smiled. "At least one of us then could have had a drink."

"Are you trying to get me drunk, Mr Twemlow?" she teased.

"Didn't think I needed to," he gave her a wink.

She felt her cheeks reddening as the waiter stepped closer. "Just an orange juice for me, please," she told him, leaning forward across the small table, twisting her fingers around each other as if unsure where to put her hands. She was suddenly so nervous, and she tried to take a deep breath and calm herself before he would notice.

"I'll have a beer," he told the waiter, who scribbled down their orders and scurried off.

He reached across the table and stilled her nervous hands.

She jumped at his touch.

"I wasn't sure if you'd come tonight," he murmured, staring down at her hands as he gently massaged her palm with his thumbs.

She raised her eyes in surprise. "Why not?"

"I wasn't sure if you'd want to see me again," he said quietly. Normally he wouldn't have cared, but this was Elsa. She had affected him in a way he couldn't quite understand.

"Did I ever give you that impression?" she was intrigued.

"No, but...well, you never can tell, can you?" he smiled, and finally looked up to meet her eye. She felt her heart skip a beat when he looked at her. She had been *dying* to see him again, how could he ever think otherwise?

She smiled as he massaged her fingers one by one, and she visibly relaxed.

"What's funny?" he asked, noticing.

"Your hands are softer than mine," she told him. "You must get through copious amounts of hand cream."

"And endless pairs of gloves," he smiled.

She gave a gentle laugh.

"So, what would you like to eat?" he asked.

She hadn't even glanced at the menu that the waiter had left them. "Anything," she grinned. "I'm *starving!*"

"On for three courses then, are you?" he challenged.

She tentatively licked her lips, and scanned down the menu. She felt herself salivating just upon reading it.

"Liver pate to start," she told him quickly, feeling her stomach rumble, "followed by hunter's chicken. Doesn't sound very French."

"They cater for everyone. You haven't even read the whole menu."

"It's OK, I eat anything," she told him with a teasing smile. "I'm not fussy."

"Thank God," he breathed, reaching forward and brushing his thumb across her bottom lip. She held his gaze in anticipation, jumping as the waiter placed a jug of water down beside them, and awkwardly snatched her hands away.

They waited while the waiter deposited bread and olives, poured their drinks and took their orders, and Elsa tried to think of something to say as she watched him stroll off.

"So, how are things at Sophia's?" Frederick asked eventually.

"Yea, not too bad," Elsa nodded enthusiastically. "Sophia's got a new horse on trial, it's not evented at all but it's done lots of unaffiliated stuff and she obviously saw something in it that she liked. It's a sweet mare," she paused, before adding, "Plus, it having no record meant that she could afford to buy it herself."

"No owners willing to plug the gap?" Frederick asked casually, not meeting her eye as he popped an olive in his mouth. She watched jealously as it passed those soft lips.

"Funnily enough we don't have owners wishing to bring Sophia their top horses, only take them away from her once she has carefully produced them," she told him coolly, and immediately cursed herself. She knew that her bitterness wasn't attractive, and she really wished that it could disappear, if only over dinner.

He looked up and met her eye, and she awkwardly looked away, not daring to try and read his closed expression.

"I'm sorry," she muttered eventually. "That was unnecessary."

"Not unnecessary," he said quietly, "If it still bothers you so."

"I really am sorry," she sighed, fighting back her eyes sudden urge to well up. "I really don't want it to bother me." As long as Nobby was happy; she wanted that to be enough for her. The rest was just business, like Sophia had said, and it had no right to interrupt her dinner.

"But?" he murmured.

"But I loved that horse so much – still do. I honestly thought he'd be at our yard forever. Him and Sophia were such a team. Despite Christine bloody Forrester's many faults, I thought even she could see what a match made in heaven they were." She broke off as she felt the lump forming in her throat.

He reached across and took her hand again. It hurt him to see her like this, and it was imperative he got to the bottom of it quickly if they were going to move this relationship to the next level, which is what he wanted – more than anything – and he hoped that she did, too. He didn't want to sneak around, worried who saw them and what they might be saying. He wanted to pick her up and spin her around, shout out to the world that she was *his*. He knew no horse could ever replace Nobby, but he wanted to tell her what he'd done for her to at least try – to prove to her that he was human, and that he *cared*.

"Please don't cry," he whispered. "It's the name of the game, Elsa. Owners can take their horses wherever they wish. Sophia is doing *really* well with the limited resources she has, and people are beginning to notice. Owners will begin to notice, and your hard work will pay off. You'll be turning owners away soon!" he gave a gentle laugh, and she forced a smile. She wished he was right.

"It's just so disheartening. I used to despair every time I saw Christine Forrester pull into the yard, forever wish she was an absent owner. Now I despair every day that she doesn't pull into the yard. Did you know she promised Sophia she would bring her a couple of youngsters, in some half-hearted attempt to replace Nobby? Yea, well there has been no sign of them."

There was silence as slowly Frederick massaged her palm. He had quickly noticed how it relaxed her so, and it was a weapon he feared he was going to need. He looked thoughtful, and she waited. Her turmoil was all his fault, and she still felt like such a traitor – to herself but especially to Sophia. She anxiously bit her lip, as she tried to put her conflicting feelings firmly out of her mind. Since forgetting how much she wanted to hate him, she was really enjoying his company. And she had really had such a fantastic night, she remembered, feeling her cheeks redden, she was very much looking forward to hopefully many more. This was one thing that was starting to go right for her, when she previously thought she could never possibly find time in her hectic life for a man, he had proved her otherwise. And she had been so happy recently. How ironic that the guy that had caused her so much heartache already this year, was the same one who had also brought her so much unexpected happiness, just from one night. Or was that two nights? Could she count the first one?

The waiter appeared quickly with their starters. Frederick reluctantly dropped her hand, and Elsa was ready – knife and fork poised – as she couldn't wait to tuck in. She tried to refrain from scoffing unattractively like a pig, like she did when it was just she and Cecil, and instead remember her manners. He was quite possibly the *poshest* person she'd ever had dinner with, after all, she realised with a small smile. Frederick picked up his fork, and hesitated. He decided now that she was mellowed with food, was a good time.

"Elsa, I have something to tell you, and I need you to not be mad at me." He began quietly, breaking her from her thoughts. Of course, he didn't think she'd be mad for very long at all – he'd acted with her happiness at the forefront of his mind – but there was no harm in a little teasing first.

She raised her eyebrows, looking at him expectantly. *Oh God, what was he going to say? That he is seeing Ava? That actually he is married?*

She took a deep breath, and waited.

"I had a visit from Christine Forrester this week." He told her, not meeting her eye.

Her breath caught. "Oh?" *Good God, he wasn't dumping her already for wretched old-hag Christine Forrester, was he?* That really would be a kick in the teeth.

"She came to talk to me about some young horses that she is

looking for a rider for." He paused. He looked up at her, and she felt her heart stop. "And I agreed to take them."

Elsa gaped at him, struggling to process what he was saying. His words met her like a kick in the stomach from a steel toe-capped boot. "You must have known she had already offered them to Sophia?" she managed to force the words out, shrouded in bitterness as her knife and fork fell to the table with a clatter.

He slowly nodded, and reached for her hand. He needed to hold her; she would understand when the whole process of events became clear. She would be *so* happy. "I had heard, yes."

She snatched her hands away, suddenly furious. She felt her world slowly but certainly collapsing around her. He had spent all this time wining and dining her, trying to get her to believe he was a decent person. And she had almost fallen for it. But not now, not now she had seen his true colours. How could he? He knew how much those horses meant to the development of her yard, and to Sophia.

"Is this how you get to where you want to be?" she spat. "By walking all over people and stabbing them in the back?"

"No, not at all," he said quietly, taken aback by her venom. "Please, let me explain?"

"What is there to explain?" she snapped.

"They are not great horses," he shook his head. "They are not going to go out and win straightaway."

"So *what*?" she demanded, trying to keep her voice down. She didn't want to draw attention to their table, but she was so angry right now. "Sophia is struggling to get runs, we needed them more than you! You take a whole lorry load to each event! But you really are a selfish pig, aren't you? You only think of yourself!"

"If you'd let me explain..." he tried, desperate to get a word in.

"Forget it! I should have known. How could you?" she

hissed. "You have decent horses coming out of your ears, you know how much a couple would mean to us – decent or not!"

"My working pupil needs a ride or two." He replied meekly, his need to explain quashed by her unexpected outburst. *A selfish pig?* The words spun in his head; he had never, *ever* been such a thing where she was concerned.

"You have *plenty*!" She replied furiously.

She wanted to hurl the stupid plastic flower and pathetic flickering candle across the small table at him, but she wasn't childish, and she definitely didn't want to make a scene.

She stopped waving her hands around, resisted folding them across her chest like a spoilt child, and instead placed them on her lap, looking down at them as she wrung her palms, anything to avoid those gorgeous blue eyes.

"Please, let me explain?" he asked gently. He needed to explain. It would all be OK; everyone would be happy.

She ignored him. She pushed her plate away, her appetite having evaporated. She didn't want to listen to anything he had to say. She should have known this was all too good to be true. He reached for her hand to calm her, if he could just massage her palm...but she snatched it away in fury.

"Elsa, please?" he ran his hand through his hair in exasperation. "Let me ex-"

"I want to go home, please," she abruptly cut him off, trying to keep the angry tears at bay.

He glared at her in disbelief, and as she met his eye she felt her anger intensifying again. *Who the hell was he to be glaring at her?* He was the one who had done wrong here. She needed to get away from him, *fast.*

He leant back in his chair, arms folded across his chest. He let out a deep sigh as he tried to work her out. She was unbelievable; he barely recognised the sweet, kind, shy, girl that he had first laid eyes on, the one he had been so drawn too. It was like she had deserted him, and been replaced with craziness. He had a perfectly good reason for his actions, he'd only done it for her, but she wouldn't even listen.

"You don't need my permission to leave," he snapped, his fight having evaporated.

Avoiding eye contact, she rose from the table, grabbed her bag and fled as fast as her wildly shaking legs would allow. She fought back the tears, ignored the lump forming in her throat as she struggled a *goodbye* to the concerned waiter. *Don't look back,* she told herself. *Never look back,* she repeated, ensuring her head was held high until she was certain she was out of view.

She leant back against the wall once outside and took a deep breath of the summer evening air, trying to calm herself before she went to her car. She was so furious, at him and at herself. She felt like such a traitor to Sophia. She felt like such a *fool*.

Her legs were still shaking as they carried her precariously back to her little, trusty Fiat. She was so grateful now that she hadn't let him pick her up. How humiliating that journey home would have been for her, if he'd have even taken her home. He could have made her get a taxi; eat into her meagre groom's wages a little more. But none of that mattered anymore. She'd trusted him, and he'd thrown that trust back in her face.

She cried as she swung the little tin can out of the car park, and headed towards the welcoming countryside. She remembered the last time he'd made her properly cry, when she'd been swinging the lorry around the country lanes, empty from having just dropped Nobby off. She had despised him then; she'd thought she could never like him. But quickly she had well and truly fallen for him, and their special night together...she sighed as she remembered how fabulous he had made her feel. She didn't think she could ever have time for a man in her life, but he had shown her she could have more than enough time for the right one.

How wrong she was about the *right one*. Now she despised him again, and she was unsure if the tears were purely because she had *really* liked him and she was so hurt by his actions, or were pure anger at herself for so easily falling for his charm and going to bed with him.

Chapter Twelve

The journey home felt like it took forever. She felt increasingly nauseas as she swung hurriedly around the twists and turns of the country lanes, desperate to be back in her cosy cottage with her main man Cecil, tucked up in her duvet and pouring her heart out to her mum on the phone.

Her tears had not subsided by the time she pulled her little car into the yard. She felt another pang of her heart as she assumed that this now automatically ended any chance of a friendship with Ava, if she was forever going to be trying to avoid Frederick at shows.

It was still light; one of the bonuses of summer evenings. But tonight it was more of a curse, as Sophia was out in the yard with her father fixing the guttering around the stable block. Sophia was perched on the top of the ladder while her father steadied the bottom, looking on amused. There was no way Elsa could get into her cottage unnoticed. Her red, puffy eyes would undoubtedly draw attention to her.

She cursed herself for being so weak, for crying over a *boy*. She was angry because it was not like her at all. But she was so hurt that he had gone so far out of his way to prove to her that he was trustworthy, to then totally betray her.

She rested her forehead on the steering wheel, trying to summon the courage to step from the car. Just when something started going right for her, something such as *business* came along and ruined it. She could see herself being single forever at this rate.

"Gosh, Elsa!" Sophia exclaimed from across the cobbles, when Elsa finally emerged from the car. "Whatever is the matter?"

"Absolutely nothing," Elsa forced a smile, her heart breaking for her; she'd have to tell her the news. "I've had a lucky escape, if anything."

"Why?" Sophia was full of concern, as she descended the ladder at breakneck speed, leaving her father behind. "What's happened? Come on, let's get you inside and the kettle on."

Her arm was around her, and she guided Elsa along the path of her cottage's tiny garden.

"It's nothing, I'm fine. Colin needs you." Elsa tried to persuade her away. She just wanted to wallow in her self-pity by herself.

"No, he doesn't," Sophia insisted. "He'd rather I left him to it, I was just trying to catch the last few rays of sun."

Elsa lifted the key from under the pot – she could never trust herself to take it out with her – and let them both in.

"Christine Forrester won't be bringing you any horses," Elsa told her sadly, leaning back against the kitchen counter as Cecil buried his head between her knees.

"Oh?" Sophia's face fell.

Elsa nodded. "Frederick is taking them, for his working pupil."

"I see," Sophia slowly nodded. This news was definitely a blow.

"He's such a prick!" Elsa sighed, letting fresh, angry tears escape. Sophia went to her, her arm around her shoulder.

"Has something else happened?" She pressed gently.

Elsa shook her head. "Isn't this bad enough?"

"You really liked him, Elsa."

"I know...I do...but..." she sobbed.

"If Christine Forrester wants to take her horses to him, he's unlikely to turn her down." Sophia forced a smile.

"He could, it would be no skin off his nose – he's got decent horses coming out of his ears," she paused as she wiped her sleeve across her puffy face. "How are you not angry?"

"I am, really I am. But well, I think I knew deep down her horses weren't coming, otherwise they'd have been here by now. And Christine can send her horses wherever she sees fit. But it's just business; if you really like him, don't let it get in the way. There'll be other horses."

"It's the principle, though." She turned away, searching the cupboards for an elusive bottle of wine. "I don't need people like him in my life."

"You need to go have a nice, long, warm shower and think this over," Sophia told her gently, trying to keep her own hurt at bay.

"There is nothing to think over," she wiped her eyes. She stopped rummaging as her hands seized a bottle of red, and stood tall. "It's done now." She told her defiantly. "It's time to move on."

She smothered the makeup wipe across her face, eager to wipe away the mascara that had smeared down her face with her tears. She ran the shower and stepped into the steaming room. Door wide open, Cecil sat watching from outside, his chin rested on his crossed paws, as if he sensed the mood was sombre.

She tried not to cry, but she felt so worn down. No matter how hard she and Sophia worked to build themselves up, something came along and tore them both back down. She felt better after a shower, pulled a towel around herself. She sat down on the edge of her bed and poured herself a large glass of wine. Cecil jumped up and snuggled beside her. She sighed as she reminisced to the special night when Frederick's glorious body had graced her bed, and tears threatened again.

She picked up her phone from the sideboard, hoping he may have tried to call, but the screen was blank. She was angry at herself, but she knew it was not she who had blown it. She wasn't going to let anyone treat her like he thought he could treat people, and she knew she must keep her head held high. She had done the right thing in walking out on him, no matter how much it hurt. Her allegiance lay with Sophia, and that was where it would always stay. She would feel better soon, maybe even in just a few days. She was strong and independent, and it wasn't like they'd really had anything in the first place. You couldn't miss what you hadn't had, could you? He was not her boyfriend; she wasn't sure that one night together even constituted a relationship.

She dried herself off and pulled on her cosy, unattractive pyjamas. She willed her phone to ring, just so she could have the small pleasure of hanging up on him. She would retain her dignity, and when he called her to explain himself and apologise, she would not give in. Cecil looked at her as though he was not quite sure he believed her. She pulled him under the duvet with her, selected her mother's number on her phone, and closed her eyes as she hit the dial button.

Slowly she prized her eyes open, hoping it had all been a horrible dream. But then the previous evenings events came flooding back to her, and it was all too vivid and real and so typical of her life to have been a dream. She had not told her mother *everything*, but enough for her mother to firmly demand that she not shed another tear over a *boy*, that there were plenty more fish in the sea, and it was preferable if she chose one who didn't dare to hurt her *little girl* in future. Elsa sighed, and Cecil rolled over and yawned, his morning dog breath escaping into her face and sending her recoiling in horror.

She crawled out of bed and pulled on her jodhpurs and t-shirt, checked her face briefly in the dusty mirror for any signs of leftover makeup smudged under her eyes. Cecil watched her with big eyes, wondering quite what had got into his mother. She rubbed his shaggy head.

"We don't need him, do we?" she forced a smile. "You were right about him all along, I guess I should have listened to you, shouldn't I?"

He whined, and she knew if he could speak he would have

given her a stern talking to, to rival her mother.

Downstairs, she put two crumpets in the toaster, gave Cecil a handful of dog biscuits, and made herself a comforting mug of strong coffee. When the crumpets sprang, she smothered them in butter, and left the cottage with her hands full, leaving the door open behind her so that Cecil could join her when his bowl was licked clean.

She quickly threw all off the feed bowls into the stables before the horses could start creating too much, and paused for a swig of coffee before she started refilling haynets. She pulled off Connor's rug and set upon him with the grooming brushes, noting she would need to clip him again later.

"Morning!" Sophia called as she strode across the yard, her eyes firmly fixed on Elsa to see what kind of mood she was in.

Elsa looked up with a smile, barely pausing from her work, and Sophia visibly relaxed.

"How are you feeling?" she asked cautiously.

"Fine, of course!" Elsa replied, as if anything at all should be the matter with her. "Connor up first?"

"Sure," Sophia nodded. "I might hack; care to bring Timber?"

"OK," Elsa nodded, knowing exactly what Sophia was up to – to get her alone and out into the fresh air of the countryside, forcing her to spill the beans of *Frederick Twemlow*. Eurgh, Elsa didn't even want to think about him right now. She definitely couldn't talk about it if she were to keep her pride.

She removed Drop Kick's rug and turned him out in the sand pen where hopefully he couldn't come to much harm. Having horses clipped out all year, there was never any reprieve from changing rugs, but at least the summer sheets were light, destined just to keep the evening chill off. There was nothing worse than lifting off and throwing on to tall horses, heavy, soaking winter rugs.

She subconsciously checked her phone. Even though she had not heard it ring, she was hopeful as she looked at the display.

But he hadn't tried to call, and she shoved it back into her pocket, vowing not to look at it again. She didn't want to talk to him, but she so wanted him to call – if only to know he still cared. But the blank screen only confirmed that he couldn't care one bit.

She cursed herself for still thinking about him as she went to the tackroom to get Bear's tack. She looked around in disdain at the state of the tackroom, stuff was thrown around everywhere, items discarded and not put back in their rightful place, which wasn't like her at all. It was just another reminder that her mind had been elsewhere recently – it certainly hadn't been one hundred percent focused on her job, which it should have been. She was normally meticulously organised where her horses were concerned; a trait that had helped her enormously since becoming a groom. She vowed to have a good clean and tidy up before their next event next week. Minty the yard cat meowed to her from the rafters, where he liked to sit and taunt Cecil, knowing that he was well out of his reach. She beckoned the hairy tabby down and tipped a handful of biscuits into his empty feed bowl on the sideboard. She looked at the kettle beside it with envy, desperate for a cup of tea alone while Sophia rode, but instead she took Bear's saddle down from the rack, and went out to fetch her in from her paddock.

Sophia was saddling up Connor, tied up in the yard. His grey coat gleamed, a testament to Elsa's hard work to always keeping Sophia's horses looking immaculate, for you never knew when a current or potential owner might spontaneously pull into the yard for a look around. This was a stark contrast to Elsa's own little mare, who lived out so that Elsa had one less stable to muck out, and was allowed to get as grubby as she liked, relishing in the fact that Elsa rarely found time to give her an absolute thorough groom. For schooling, Elsa brushed where the saddle and bridle went, and for hacking away from the yard she brushed enough of the dirt off so that she would not bring the yard into disrepute.

They headed out across the farmland in silence, and Elsa waited for Sophia to begin the questioning that she knew she was so desperate to ask. Bear excitedly chomped on her bit and shook her head, breaking into a jog every now and then, with Elsa quickly insisting she walked.

"She's looking well," Sophia commented, with a smile.

"She's definitely feeling very well," Elsa replied. "Think she could do with a few more runs to settle her down a bit."

"Well, my season isn't exactly going to plan, so you may as well make the most of the gaps in my calendar and get her out and about as much as you can."

"Every cloud and all that," Elsa nodded desolately, because no one missed going to events as much as she did. She loved showing off her horses and seeing Sophia the underdog storm into contention.

They trotted the length of a sheep paddock, before pushing the horses into a canter further along the valley. It was so quiet, but even on a still day such as today, the wind howled in their ears as they picked up the pace. They were surrounded by rolling hills, and it was Elsa's most favourite place on earth, out here on a horse. You could totally lose track of time and hack for miles and miles and not encounter a car, but did come across the occasional farmstead or hiker. However, it was not so idyllic when your mount decided to dump you and you had to find your own way home from God-knows-where, as Elsa had experienced only once. Her stick-ability had dramatically improved overnight since that inauspicious day.

"I really want to get her out to some cross-country schooling," Elsa commented as they eased to a walk. She had been thinking about it a lot all morning, and liked already how planning her competitive future with Bear had cheered her up immensely. "Maybe even take her show jumping. Anything to get the excitement of cross country concealed a little."

"She'll calm down the more she does it," Sophia agreed.

They walked in silence for a moment. Elsa chewed her lip. "Frederick even invited us over to use his course," she said eventually. "You know, before...well, you know."

"No, I don't actually," Sophia replied kindly. "What happened, Elsa? What was *actually* going on – were you properly together, or what? And what the hell went so wrong? You seemed to really like him."

"He's a liar," Elsa shrugged. "A selfish liar, he only cares about himself."

"I'm not his biggest fan, but I don't believe that is totally true," Sophia replied dubiously. "He's very highly thought of by his fellow competitors. And I don't believe that he invites many people over to school over his cross-country course. He comes across as very private."

"Well, it doesn't matter now anyway, does it?" Elsa replied, trying to conceal her sadness. He still had not called. How long did you leave it after a row to decide that he really wasn't going to call?

The tackroom was undeniably requiring Elsa's attention, and she donned her shorts and a vest top and set about the back breaking task of emptying its contents out onto the yard. This was always her preferred method of tidying; to empty out a room completely, and only put items back once they were clean and boxed away nicely. Plus, while the contents were scattered across the yard, Elsa could not go home until the task was finished. It was the method that she took with the lorry at the end of the eventing season; emptying the whole thing out. Otherwise it just got left and forgotten about, and this way there was no mouldy surprises at the start of the new season, when she opened a tack locker and found a pile of festering, muddy, sweaty bandages.

"You're very thorough, Elsa," Sophia commented on passing

the mountain of equipment clogging up her yard. Her treasured groom was brushing the cobwebs and dust from each numnah, and rearranged them in neat, colour-coordinated piles.

"Of course! You know me," she smiled, disappearing back inside and reappearing dragging out a filthy mud-covered heavyweight turnout rug and adding it to the rugs-to-be-washed-before-winter-set-in pile. She wondered how she had missed that one; the heavyweight rugs were normally washed as soon as the horses no longer required them – usually in spring – and packed away ready for the next bout of horrid weather.

She found all cleaning tasks quite therapeutic; good thinking time and a chance for reflection. However, having time to clean mid-way through the eventing season was not a good sign; it was an indication that they didn't have enough horses in work or enough events to attend, which was frustrating.

Normally, cleaning and maintenance jobs were reserved for winter when most of the horses were turned out at grass, in anticipation of a busy eventing season ahead. Last winter when she had cleaned, repaired the broken fences and repainted the stable doors, they had both had such high hopes for the season ahead. Most of those hopes laid with Nobby. Her heart panged for him. What she wouldn't give to have his kind face gazing out over the top of his old stable door.

Frederick-bloody-Twemlow, she cursed. She had been doing so well at not thinking about him, but there was always something that brought him flooding back into her mind, clouding her thoughts and rousing her anger. She was just glad that she had so many things still to do, that it was not too hard to tear her mind back to where it should be.

Connor had got quite warm while Sophia worked him, and Elsa noticed that he had sweated up quite a bit along the neck and front. She unsaddled him and left him in the yard while she went to find the clippers. He pawed at the ground impatiently, wondering why he wasn't being turned straight out.

The one thing Elsa hated about clipping, was having to wear waterproofs on a nice, hot day, and still getting clumps of hair in the places you'd least expect it. She itched all over, and couldn't wait to get inside and jump straight in the shower. She shivered uncomfortably, irritably brushed some clumps of grey hair out from beneath her sweaty bra, wondering how the hell they got there, and how the hell such tiny hair could prick your skin like pins.

She was desperate to get inside for an ice-cool drink and a cold shower, and a quick check of the water butts – praying for no empty ones – was the only thing that stood in her way.

Elsa groaned as she peered over Drop Kick's door. The grey gelding stood motionlessly at the back of his stable, looking sheepish.

"I know you are fed up of box rest," Elsa told him sternly, referring to the fresh droppings swimming in his water bucket. "But really must you be so rebellious?"

He gave her an affectionate nuzzle, and she couldn't stay angry for long. She dragged the bucket across the freshly-swept cobbles, and tipped its contents down the drain.

She had just located a stiff brush and started giving it a meaningful scrub, when the unknown car pulled into the yard. It was just an average car, not one that stood out. Not too flash and definitely not a banger like her Fiat. She didn't recognise it, or the man driving, and he pulled to a halt and slowly climbed out.

He was well dressed, wearing a beige checked shirt with a loose, tweed waistcoat, corduroy trousers and worn, brown laced shoes with slightly scuffed toes. He looked as though he were in his late fifties, with thin, neat blonde hair that hid well the tints of grey at the sides.

He regarded Elsa for a moment, and she waited, brush poised as though his words were well anticipated.

"I am hoping this is Sophia Hamilton's stables," he spoke eventually, his middle-class voice smooth and kind.

"Yes, it is," Elsa replied, standing, and waited as he looked around himself, and she couldn't decide whether it was a look of admiration or dislike.

Eventually his grey eyes fell on her again. "Please may I speak with her?"

"I'm afraid she's out hacking one of the youngsters at the moment." Elsa told him, intrigued by their visitor. "Is she expecting you?"

"No, she isn't," he paused briefly for another gaze over his surroundings, and seemed satisfied. "But I can wait."

"I'm Elsa, her Head Girl. Is it anything I can help you with?"

"Sorry," he smiled, stepping towards her and outstretching his hand to her. "How foolish of me not to introduce myself. My name is Michael Patricks."

Elsa duly shook his hand, trying to figure out where she might recognise the strangers name from.

"I have horses with Frederick Twemlow," he helped her out.

Bingo. Her breath caught. *Frederick Twemlow.* She took a deep breath and had to momentarily look away. They were good horses, too, if she remembered correctly, so why was he here?

"Or at least I did," he added.

"Oh?" she looked up sharply. She involuntarily dropped her brush to the cobbles and folded her arms across her chest; he had her undivided attention.

"Unfortunately, we have parted company; there are no hard feelings and it is nothing that the horses or Fred has done wrong. Fred is at the top of his game, and all of his horses are brilliant, so I just felt that mine were getting a bit left behind. Fred admitted that they probably wouldn't get the runs that I had hoped for next season as he focuses on the titles. I offered them to his working pupil, but he said my horses were more of a lady's ride and insisted I bring them to Sophia. I just hope she'll take them."

Elsa's heart was in her mouth as she absorbed what he was saying. "He *insisted?*" she repeated, the words sticking in her throat.

"Oh yes, he's very fair and honest." Michael went on. "I was more than happy for his working pupil to have them, but he is adamant Sophia is the best young rider around. He spoke very highly of her and I would be privileged if she would consider taking my string under her wing. It was a promising conversation, I'm very much excited about their futures now."

Elsa brushed her hair back from her face, and nervously bit on her lower lip as she tried to piece together what had happened.

"When exactly was this conversation?" she asked him, the timing suddenly very important.

"Last week," Michael replied, not giving it too much thought. "Possibly Monday? I meant to come here sooner, but a new business deal got in the way. You know, business takes priority. The horses are just a hobby for me."

Elsa nodded in understanding as she tried to process this series of events. Keeping event horses was an expensive game, and the owners often worked very hard outside of the horse world to fund their privileged hobby.

Her face was as white as a sheet. She rubbed a clammy palm over her stomach as she contemplated throwing up; the sudden feeling of nausea was overwhelming.

They had had that conversation before Frederick had met her for dinner, so this wasn't his attempt at an apology. *Because he didn't owe her an apology.*

Instead, she had spoken to him with absolute contempt without even drawing breath to let him explain that actually he had orchestrated something so beautifully generous for them.

She had walked out on him. She felt awful as her mind went back over the events of that evening that she had tried so desperately to forget. *What the hell had she done?*

"Are you alright?" Michael narrowed concerned eyes at her.

Quickly she nodded, remembering her manners. "Can I get you a drink while you wait?" she ushered him towards the tackroom. "A tea? Or a coffee?"

Frederick had used his power and generosity to land them an amazing catch, and there was no way she was going to mess this up for Sophia.

Elsa could barely keep still while they waited for Sophia to return. He sat easily, nursing his tea and curiously watching her as she subtly paced the room and attempted to make conversation with her.

As soon as Elsa heard hooves in the yard she had sprinted from the tackroom and taken Ruby's reins, and was shoving Sophia towards their visitor.

"Bit of a turnaround, isn't it?" Sophia murmured, once she had finished with him, and the pair of them watched his car amble away back down the drive.

Elsa squatted on the gravel, her face in her palms. While tending to Ruby, she had gone over and over her last conversation with Frederick, and every time she replayed it, it appeared worse than she previously remembered.

"Did you know about this?" Sophia asked gently.

"I had no idea," she shook her head, it never leaving her hands as she struggled to fight back angry tears. She was furious at herself.

"I'm surprised he didn't tell you," Sophia frowned.

"He tried," Elsa cut her off, eventually looking at her. "Looking back, I think he tried. But I wouldn't listen. I was *so* rude to him, Soph."

"You were always stubborn, Elsa," Sophia bit her lip.

Elsa watched her, waiting. She wanted Sophia to tell her she had done the right thing, speaking to him the way she had. That he deserved it, that he should have tried harder to explain while she was biting his head off. But she knew they would be lies.

"Frederick only took Christine Forrester's youngsters so that he could send us two better ones," she murmured. "I've really messed up, haven't I?"

Slowly, Sophia nodded. "As much as I hate to admit it, I think you might have, yes."

"For fuck sake!" she slammed her fist down against the unforgiving gravel in a rare burst of anger. "Me and my *stupid* big mouth! I just automatically assumed he was screwing us over."

She ran her hands through her hair in exasperation as she replayed that fateful dinner date scene again. *Stop it!* She told herself harshly.

"And why do you think he would do that?" Sophia asked gently.

"He wouldn't," Elsa admitted, finally seeing it, as her voice turned to a whisper. "I know now, he wouldn't. And I wouldn't even let him explain," she sighed. "I wouldn't hear him out. I'm such a *fool!*"

"Have you heard from him since?" Sophia asked cautiously.

"Not a bean," Elsa shook her head, and nervously clamped her bottom lip between her teeth. "It's not looking good, is it? And I know it's exactly what I deserve."

There was a pause, as Sophia diplomatically chose her words. "If you like him, then you need to get around there and see him."

Elsa slowly shook her head, feeling her stomach churn with longing. "He'd never see me – not now – not after everything that I called him."

"It doesn't matter; if you really like him, you have to at least try. And I have a thank you card to write to him." Sophia gave a gentle smile. "Michael Patrick's horses are extremely underrated. They could be our next Nobby."

Chapter Thirteen

Elsa saddled Red the pony for his final ride with Sophia before it was time for him to return home. He was a sweet gelding, a fiery chestnut colour to match his name, only fourteen hands high but Sophia didn't look too big on him, and Elsa even less so. He was quite chunky and carried a larger adult easily. But his excessive enthusiasm towards his work had gotten the better of him recently, and he had run away with his teenage owner a couple of times, and so the teenagers mother had sent him to Sophia to be reminded of his manners.

Elsa had done most of the work with him, and she absolutely adored him. He was the ultimate fun pony who would try his hoof at anything, but she was happy that he was ready to return home, as his owner had been missing him terribly.

"I'm going to take him over to the gallops," Sophia told her as she took his reins. "Hopefully they'll be other horses about and I can let him go and really test his brakes without a horse by his side to nanny him."

Elsa nodded. "Good idea. I don't think the poor girl could cope with him running off again." He had only done it once with Elsa, when he had very first arrived two weeks previous, but they had quickly found him another bit that suited him better, and that combined with some intensive schooling with a variety of exercises, and he had not even thought about it since.

"He'll be absolutely fine," Elsa reaffirmed. "How long will you be? I'll have Connor ready for when you get back."

But Sophia noticed the shadow of the desolate look she had been trying so hard to conceal over the past few days.

"How about you just give him a quick brush and I'll do the

rest myself?" she smiled gently. "You get out of here and go and see that boy."

"You think that's a good idea?" Elsa nervously bit her lip. She had been contemplating going to see Frederick, ever since he wouldn't answer his phone, but she didn't want to look like his newest stalker. "I know I have got some apologising to do, but I wouldn't blame him if he doesn't want to listen."

"Depends whether you want him back or not?" Sophia shrugged. "It's got to be a worth a shot if you like him?"

Like him? Elsa mulled. It was a feeling much stronger than that, one that she couldn't quite put into words, but one that kept her awake at night, led her focus astray in the daytime. She knew she wasn't going to snap out of this until she had seen him. It wasn't going to just go away. It really was worth a shot, wasn't it? Her mind would never rest until she had at least tried to make amends with him.

She checked that all the horses had enough hay and water to last the afternoon, and dashed back to her little cottage as fast as her legs would allow. Cecil trotted along behind, wondering what the sudden rush was all about. Elsa knew that he wouldn't approve, were she to tell him, so instead she threw him a chewy treat to keep him quiet and jumped in the shower. She wanted to get over there, find him and say her piece before she had a chance to talk herself out of it.

What had they even had, though? Elsa wondered as she scrubbed her skin red raw under the steaming water, wanting to rid herself of any hint of the scent of horse. Had they had *anything*? Did she have any right to grieve not having it now? She was sure they'd had more than just a one-night stand because he'd been keen to see her again. He'd always been keen to see her, though; it was she who had been calling the shots, until now. She had felt very much on the backfoot since he hadn't even called. She really wished he would.

She gave a hollow laugh as she remembered back to the time she'd not wanted him to notice her while she watched Nobby do his first dressage test under his new rider, how she hadn't wanted to bump into him at his own yard when most girls would sell their vital organs if it meant they could get that opportunity. That seemed like such a long time ago, but it really wasn't. She couldn't believe someone who she hadn't even liked in the beginning could put her mind into turmoil in such a short space of time.

He was all she thought about. She'd lost her appetite, her focus. Her job was suffering although she did well to conceal that. But she couldn't have concealed the happiness he'd made her feel, like now she could not conceal her sadness. All because of Frederick. Well, a little because of her big mouth, but that was still because of Frederick.

She ran the razor over her legs, and tried her hardest to calm her nervous, shaking hands before she guided the blade along her bikini line. She wondered if this time she really was being optimistic, but it made her feel better at least.

She dried herself off and rummaged impatiently through her wardrobe for something nice to wear. Half of the clothes that occupied it she never had a chance to wear, but her eyes settled on a flowery jumpsuit that she had worn a couple of times previously, and remembered the comments of approval it had received. She put a layer of mascara on – and hoped she would remember she was wearing it and not smudge it into her face – but that was all. She wanted to look nice for him; she didn't want to look desperate or over the top, but just something to say "look, I'm here and looking pretty" rather than just blending in as another groom. She had spent so long just trying to blend in as a groom as Sophia climbed the ranks and Elsa joined superior company, she was apprehensive about this opportunity she must now take to stand out. Now was not the time to be *just a groom*.

Elsa rolled her noisy, rattling little Fiat up to the grand front gates of the Twemlow's tranquil estate, and took a deep breath. She had almost turned around several times on her way here, certain he would not forgive her, but knowing that she would never forgive herself if she didn't try.

She desperately hoped he was in; she had checked the calendar and there were no events on today, or local clinics that she knew of. Frederick's clinics were well talked about – she would have heard about it were he holding one. She had been going over and over in her head what she was going to say to him, and she had her speech prepared to perfection, yet she knew that as soon as she laid eyes on him she'd be so tongue-tied she'd struggle with every single word.

But what if he won't see me? Her heart lurched. But surely he would. Of course he would, he was Frederick, the one who had become so persistent to get to know her.

Yes, there was no way he wouldn't see her. She just hoped he would forgive her for leaving it so long.

Her hands were sweating as they clutched the steering wheel. Gathering herself, she popped the Fiat into first gear, and slowly eased it up the pristine gravel drive towards the stable block.

She pulled to a halt beside Frederick's lavish lorry, and looked around for any sign of Ava before she got out. She wished she could see her, she could pour her heart out to her and Ava would laugh and tell her exactly what she needed to do to make it right with Frederick. But she was nowhere to be seen, and a redheaded girl paused from brushing off a big bay tied in the yard, and regarded her with suspicion. Of course, Elsa appreciated that her battered Fiat immediately gave away that she could not possibly be an owner, or anyone else of influence or importance, and therefore she should probably not be worthy of any of Frederick Twemlow's *precious* time, she thought bitterly. Frederick's grooms were probably used to fending off crazed women; they probably had impeccable guard dog techniques.

She took a deep breath and climbed out from the car. The

redhead was still watching her, and Elsa approached her confidently, as if she had every right to be here.

"Morning!" she called cheerfully. "I'm here to see Frederick."

"Is he expecting you?" The redhead asked from under raised eyebrows, obviously immediately detecting a fraud.

"Of course!" Elsa waved her hand breezily, as if they were old friends and she came here to see him *all* the time. Her bashfulness surprised even herself, and displayed nothing of the nausea she was feeling. "Shall I just go on through?"

Through to where, she had no idea, but it didn't matter, because at that moment she saw him crossing the yard before her, not noticing her as he appeared to be deep in thought. He looked so natural in his grey breeches, long black leather boots, and pastel polo shirt. But then he looked up, met her eye, and she waited, anxiously biting her lip as she wondered which of them would speak first. But he wasn't stopping, and there was no familiar smile tugging at those soft lips.

"Frederick!" she called after him frantically, and for a split second he stopped and looked at her again. But she could not diminish the anguished expression that fleetingly skipped across his face before being replaced with something more gut wrenching yet unrecognisable to her, and he turned and continued hurriedly on his way.

Despair? Disappointment? Fear?

She stood rooted to the spot, looking after him as he disappeared around the corner, and she heard a door slam behind him.

She hurried across the spotless concrete yard after him, and tried the door, but it would not budge. She had not heard it lock, and she imagined him leaning the bulk of his weight against it, preventing her from reaching him.

You only have one chance, Elsa. Give it your best. She took a deep breath.

"Frederick," she whispered, tapping feebly on the door, and she cleared her throat. "I need to say sorry. I've really messed up. I didn't give you a chance to explain, I just jumped to conclusions – typical me – and I said some unforgiveable things." She paused. He was still there, she knew he was, and she was sure if she stayed really quiet she could even hear him breathing.

"You've shown me nothing but kindness, and you didn't deserve...the way I *behaved* towards you. I really need to apologise." She let her head bang against the door in frustration. She'd had so much she wanted to say to him, yet the only time it mattered and the words would not come to her.

"I haven't even known you that long, but I feel like I've known you forever. And well, I miss you, Fred. I *really* miss you."

He sighed. *Fred*. She had never called him that before, it was always Frederick. Everyone called him Fred, except her. Well, and his mother, but he didn't want to think about *her* right now. She was always telling him he was over sensitive.

She'd missed him? But had she really? Had she been missing him while she thought him to be the most dishonest human being gracing this planet?

He loved the way she said *Frederick*, he realised longingly. Her sweet, soft, cheerful voice that could brighten up the dullest of days. And that *smile*, he tormented himself. She really did have such a beautiful smile, but not while she was snarling at him across the dinner table.

Her words had cut through him like a knife. The hurt was still raw. He was fed up of people thinking wrongly of him, and it hurt even more so because it was her. He'd thought she was different. He'd always been honest with her; what she saw of him was what she'd got, he'd never kept anything hidden. He was not a *selfish pig*, he painfully remembered her words, and he had never trodden on *anyone* to get what he wanted.

"I remember at Napier, my mind was in such a turmoil," she

spoke so quietly, he strained to listen. "I so desperately wanted to hate you for stealing Nobby, but how could I? You were so intent on making me laugh and smile and *like* you, but you're so…naturally loveable." She smiled. "I wanted you to kiss me so much. But you wouldn't."

She gently touched her lips, remembering the feel of him against them. *Just open this bloody door and kiss me!* Her heart screamed, but it did not even flinch.

"When you turned up at Bear's event, I wanted the ground to open up and swallow me whole. I never imagined you could be there for me. But well, I think that was the best I have possibly ever ridden in my entire life – and the worst, because my mind was on you the whole time. My mind is always on you, Frederick."

Frederick. He sighed, remembering how sweetly she cried out his name in her bed while he was bringing her to multiple orgasms, and he wanted to drive his fist into the door in frustration. He would never be enough for her, he knew that. He had given her his whole being, and still she had thought he was shielding things, that he was dishonest. He couldn't give her any more than everything.

"When you helped me out that day, when you offered for me to bring Bear schooling over your fences, I felt so honoured that you would give up such precious time for me. I wondered what you could possibly see in me, I guess I have always wondered that since the very start. I'm just a groom, after all, and Bear and I will never be at the dizzying heights that you are at. We can dream, of course, but I'm more of a realist. So, I always thought it was too good to be true, that *you* could possibly like *me*, and there had to be an ulterior motive. The more I saw you, the more turmoil my mind was in. I guess I should have trusted you."

Guess? She didn't sound too convinced, he detected.

"I miss you so much, Frederick," she whispered. "Please, open the door?"

He couldn't take much more of this. Did she miss him because of the opportunities she thought he could provide, to better her career? The free coaching? Was she really as shallow as the rest of them? He was fed up of girls thinking that – and there had been plenty. She should have trusted him, but ultimately, she hadn't. Instead she had shown her true colours, and it hurt desperately what she truly thought of him. But her lack of self-confidence really narked at him. *Just a groom?* She could be anyone she wanted to be, she didn't need him. And she had already shown she didn't really want him. It had been agony for him, every day that had passed since that horrible evening, and he didn't get to see her. He had not realised before, the extent to which she brightened up his day. But he couldn't forget her anger, her hatred towards him, her *words*. If she was here just to make him feel better, he didn't need her sympathy. Maybe she was just here to make herself feel better…he couldn't deal with this. He could never tell her now, just quite how much she had meant to him.

The door swung open and she almost fell into the room. She picked herself hastily up and met those beautiful eyes staring down at her, with a gasp.

"Don't you ever say you are *just a groom*, Elsa," he snapped. He looked so *hurt*, she longed to reach out and touch him, to trail a gentle finger down his cheek.

There was no time to implore with him, for him to look her properly in the eye – and see how badly she meant what she said, before the door was slammed shut, and she heard the definitive footsteps of him leaving her. She sighed; it was so tempting just to grab the door handle and chase after him, but what would it achieve?

She had said all she needed to say, and her heart panged. She wanted so badly to see him, that carefree smile, not the anguished look she'd just received a fleeting glance of. She wanted to hold him in her hands and force him to look at her. Maybe if he looked back at her, met her eye for eye, he'd see just how sorry she was. But she wouldn't chase something who clearly thought so little of her to allow her that chance to explain.

"What's this about, Elsa?" came Ava's gentle, friendly voice, filled with empathy and making her jump. Elsa wondered if she had been standing behind her the whole time. The look on the Australian's face confirmed that she had.

"I need to *see* him," Elsa persisted. She was sure if he could look her properly in the eye, if he'd just *look* at her while she explained – he'd see how sorry she was – how much she meant her words.

"I can't make him, Elsa. He doesn't see many people," Ava shrugged. "Unless they're important – like owners or whatever."

"Guess I'm just not important, huh?" Elsa fought back tears.

"By his reaction, I'd guess that you were," she told her sadly. "He's sensitive."

Were. Past tense. Elsa sighed. Maybe she had been important to him once, but she certainly wasn't any more.

"So, was he the guy you were going for dinner with, that night at Picton?" Ava probed. "The one you *swore* wasn't a date?"

Slowly Elsa nodded.

"Wow, I honestly had no idea at the time. Suppose it makes sense now, though." She forced a gentle smile. "Although, Fred's reaction when he saw you in that dress, he sure played it cool."

"He knew it was your dress," Elsa smiled fondly, desperately trying to keep her tears of humiliation at bay.

"Of course he would," Ava nodded. "Nothing much gets past him."

Elsa took a deep breath. She had to ask and it was now or never. "Were you and him ever – you know?"

"No way, Elsa!" Ava looked offended. "He's my boss – *just* my boss. And I don't go in for the whole leering over my boss thing."

"I just wondered," she shrugged, suddenly embarrassed. "It's just he said you go to a lot of things with him."

"Yea, because he knows I won't have a bit too much to drink and throw myself at him," Ava laughed. She had been asked the question a thousand times, she should be used to it by now. "He's safe with me, and I with him. I can divert unwanted female attention, and chat away with owners about the horses."

Elsa nodded. There was silence as her mind tried to absorb the situation. She understood so much now; she could see things so much clearer. "I wanted to hate him so much for taking Nobby..." she broke off; it was pointless going over this old ground.

"For the record," Ava added, feeling like she had to get this one out there, "Fred never *stole* Nobby. Truth be told, he didn't really want him. He's a lovely horse, but he was Sophia's lovely horse, and Fred gets no joy from accepting horses that are already performing well for other riders."

She paused, and Elsa felt any remaining colour drain from her face. She felt her heart slow. *Was Ava being serious?*

Slowly Ava nodded, as if reading her mind. "Fred gets his kicks from taking on underperforming and unwanted horses, difficult even. Not ones like Nobby. But that bloody woman was persistent; she was round here most days insisting how miserable Nobby was at Sophia's and imploring with us to take him. I should know; I bore the brunt of most of her visits. We knew how much you must dislike her, and Fred thought her behaviour towards you was despicable. So, when he heard you were having her youngsters, he thought he'd save you from having her ever set foot in your yard again."

Elsa felt sick, but slowly she nodded as she absorbed Ava's words. "So, he promised to take the youngsters, but had to free up two stables, so he sent us Michael Patricks?"

"They are good horses," Ava nodded. "Much better than

Forrester's. He thought Sophia deserved a couple of decent horses to get her back on track. He didn't trust Christine Forrester not to take her youngsters away from you once they were going nicely; Michael would never do that."

Elsa crouched to the ground, taking deep breaths. She needed to calm herself before she could trust herself to walk or speak again. She was so full of hatred towards Christine Forrester, but not surprised that she had bad-mouthed Sophia to climb the social ladder. Frederick would never have believed her. *She should have trusted him.*

"I've really messed up," she murmured, her head in her hands.

"It's an easy mistake to make," Ava tried to comfort her. "You weren't to know."

"He tried to tell me," Elsa told her sadly, fighting back fresh tears. "I wouldn't listen. I'm not sure he'll ever forgive me."

"Give him some time," Ava told her gently, waiting in silence until Elsa found the strength to stand. Eventually she collected her thoughts, and rose to meet her. She just wanted to get back to the comfort of her own yard.

"Does this mean you're going to avoid me at events now?" Ava teased.

"I hope not," Elsa cracked the first genuine smile she had managed all week. "I was hoping we could still be friends?"

"Of course, kid. You could have told me, you know?"

"What was there to tell?" Elsa shrugged. "He kept asking me to dinner, I kept refusing because I had totally the wrong idea about him. I finally give in but by the time I realise I actually quite like him, it's too late?"

"How the hell did you manage to mess things up quite so much?" Ava was genuinely intrigued.

"Oh, it's my speciality!" she replied, with a roll of her eyes, and through her sadness they both managed a gentle laugh.

"I should have listened to you about him," she told her sadly. "I shouldn't have been so hostile."

Slowly Ava nodded. "He's sensitive. *Very* sensitive, and very loyal. And everything I told you about what a nice person he is, it is true. He is a lovely, kind-hearted person."

"I know that *now*," she hastily wiped at an escaped tear.

"Come here," Ava put her arm around her, and Elsa allowed the tears to escape and soak into the Australian's t-shirt.

"I really shouldn't be crying over a guy," Elsa snivelled in embarrassment. "It is really not like me at all."

"How about I get you a cup of tea?" Ava grinned. "You Brits seem to solve everything with a cup of tea, right?"

"I think it's going to take something a bit stronger than a cup of tea," Elsa wiped her face, hoping that Frederick didn't decide to walk back around the corner now her face was red and blotchy, and surely her mascara had run.

She looked at Ava, as if hoping for an answer to solve this huge mess she'd created for herself.

"Just give him time, maybe?" Ava repeated confidently. Her heart broke for the pair of them. She'd come to both greatly admire and respect Fred in the five years she'd known him. Although she'd never have put the two of them together, she didn't doubt for one minute they had something; she had never seen him act so venomously towards a girl before. If anyone deserved to be happy, it was Fred. Wealth and status didn't automatically guarantee happiness, and behind his *Mr Cool* façade, she knew better than anyone that Fred was a prime example of that. In the short time she had known Elsa, she'd come to think of her as a strong friend, and she would like nothing more than to see the pair of them happy together. But they were both proud and stubborn. She figured the pair of them could be the perfect match, and she felt that if they clearly felt so strongly about each other, they would be certain to figure something out.

Elsa nodded, as if finally accepting that she had no other choice than to give it time. "I'd better be going. Sorry for..."

"Hey, don't apologise," Ava cut her off. "How about we hit

the town Friday night, hey? Let your hair down, try and take your mind off it? Let's hang out away from horses for a change!"

Elsa nodded. "Yea, I'd really like that."

"Great!" Ava winked. "That's a date, then!"

"Yes!" Elsa nodded enthusiastically. "And I might even be able to find my own dress to wear!"

With a parting hug, she ambled back across the gravel to her trusty Fiat. She walked slowly, giving Frederick his last chance to come hurtling out after her, and give her another chance. She even dragged her feet subtly to make certain that he'd hear her cross the noisy gravel. She let out a sigh as she reached the Fiat. There was no sign of Frederick, and she knew she'd blown it. She continued to force the smile while she waved farewell to Ava, and headed down the drive. And then the smile fell, along with the tears of frustration and anger at herself, and she allowed herself this last, final cry over the relationship that never was, before she told herself to pull it together, and get over it.

She had messed up, and there was nothing she could do *but* get over it. If he would not answer her calls, and would not see her, then she couldn't continue to chase him or she'd get locked up for being an obsessive stalker. And she didn't want to be one of *those girls* that chased him around events doing anything to get his attention.

Elsa had never known a drive back to the yard feeling quite so long as that one. Not even the one when she had dropped Nobby off. *Nobby,* she sighed, she had not even got a chance to see *him.* She clenched and unclenched her palms around the steering wheel, and made sure her eyes were dry and her face had resumed to its normal whiteness before she pulled back up to her little cottage.

She made herself a cup of tea – resisting opening a bottle of wine so early in the day – and let Cecil curl up on her lap as she drank it on the sofa. He sensed something was wrong, and licked her face as if to make it better.

"We're going to be OK, fella," she told him, scratching behind his ears. "I'm stronger than that. There's no room for negative thoughts in my life, is there?"

He whined as she spoke to him, and she smiled. The cottage was so quiet and peaceful, she could easily fall asleep if she sat here for too long. She dropped Cecil to the floor and stood up, assessing the beautiful view of the valleys that her living room window was graced with, and it filled her with an irreplaceable pleasure. She had everything she could ever possibly want; a home in one of the most beautiful places in the world, a job she loved, endless four-legged best friends, and an employer who was much more than just a boss. She knew that some would argue she was the luckiest girl in the world. She turned to look at herself in the mirror, and plastered on her best smile.

"That's better," she said out loud. "Now time to get these silly clothes off, and back out to what I do best."

"How did it go?" Sophia asked, from where she hosed Connor off in the yard. Elsa walked briskly and purposefully. Sophia cautiously regarded the fact that she hadn't been gone very long, and had already changed back into her jodhpurs, but she remained hopeful all the same.

A stern shake of Elsa's head quickly cut her off, and Sophia's optimistic smile fell from her face.

"*Oh.*"

"It's fine," Elsa insisted, taking a deep breath, she slung two haynets over her shoulder. "I'm fine... by myself. In fact, I am more than fine. I have Cecil, I have you, this place, a job that I love, and a nice home. I don't *need* anything else. And I'm going to be fine, OK?"

Sophia nodded. "Of course you are; I wouldn't expect anything less from you."

"Good," she smiled. A genuine, start of a real smile. "So, who's up next? What do you want me to do?"

"Well," Sophia wrung her hands together nervously. "Michael Patricks rang, he said his horses are ready to come over tomorrow. I said you'd fetch them, but apparently Frederick insisted that one of his grooms will bring them."

Else felt her heart pang, and took a deep breath. It felt like a knife to the heart that he obviously *really* didn't want to see her, but she held her composure despite it being so painful. Of course, she would be fine on her own, but she didn't intend to be on her own for long. Because she would show him. She could give him time, and space, and she would wait. Some things were worth the wait, and she knew he was one of them. And she wasn't going to give up. If he wanted a fight, he would get one, because she would fight to her death to show him how sorry she was, and just how much he meant to her. She just needed to configure a plan to make it all come together. And she would think of one, because there was no way she was prepared to let him go that easily.

"That's fine," she replied, her voice cracking, and she cleared her throat. "I'll get their stables ready."

"Elsa..."

"It's fine," she insisted with a smile, enthusiastically grabbing a pitch fork. "I told you, everything is fine. Onwards and upwards. Things are going to start looking up for us, Sophia. For the both of us, I can just feel it – and these two new horses are going to be the key. Let's keep looking forwards; we can't do anything about the past."

Just a groom. There was no way she was simply that; she was the life-blood of this yard. She was groom, exercise rider, multi-tasker, lorry driver, best friend, idea sounding board, counsellor, the one that picked them up when things weren't going to plan. Sophia needed her, and Elsa needed Sophia now more than ever. Together, they formed the *best* team, and together they were going to travel all over the world, and conquer the eventing ranks.

About the Author

Laurie Twizel lives and breathes horses. When not writing, she can often be found roaming the beautiful countryside of her current home in the South East of England, with or without a horse!

Follow her on social media for all the latest book releases
"Laurie Twizel – Author"
@LaurieTwizel
Blog – http://laurietwizel.blogspot.co.uk

If you enjoyed this book, please let your friends know! Laurie would also love your feedback; you can drop her an email
at laurie.twizel@gmail.com

Printed in Great Britain
by Amazon